"That's blackmail!"

"Not at all," he said, "just sound business practice."

"That's pretty low, Stephen," she bit out. "Even for you."

"Oh come on, Rachel. I didn't say I was going to do it. But if his one employee can only be obstructive and uncooperative, snapping at the hand that just might feed her…" He shrugged. "What else can a man do?"

Rosemary Hammond grew up in California, but has since lived in several other states. Rosemary and her husband have traveled extensively throughout the United States, Mexico, the Caribbean and Canada, both with and without their two sons. She enjoys gardening, music and needlework, but her greatest pleasure has always been reading. She started writing romances because she enjoyed them, but also because the mechanics of fiction fascinated her and she thought they might be something she could do.

Books by Rosemary Hammond

ALL IT TAKES IS LOVE
Rosemary Hammond

Harlequin Books

TORONTO • NEW YORK • LONDON
AMSTERDAM • PARIS • SYDNEY • HAMBURG
STOCKHOLM • ATHENS • TOKYO • MILAN
MADRID • WARSAW • BUDAPEST • AUCKLAND

ISBN 0-373-03357-5

ALL IT TAKES IS LOVE

Copyright © 1993 by Rosemary Hammond.

First North American Publication 1995.

CHAPTER ONE

IT WAS unseasonably warm for Seattle in April, and, as Rachel walked the half-block from the bus-stop to her office, she already regretted the woollen suit she'd worn that morning. Although there was a breeze blowing off Puget Sound, just a few blocks down the hill to the west, it was a decidedly balmy one.

The small publishing company she worked for was located in Pioneer Square, on the fringes of the old Skid Road area, long since renovated, and sandwiched in between an art gallery and a law office. She'd come into work early that morning on a special summons from her boss, who had called her late last night, assuring her it was a matter of some urgency.

'Good morning, Sam,' she said as she entered the tiny reception room. She stifled a yawn. 'This had better be good. I'm not used to such early hours.'

He was lounging in the one visitor's chair, flipping through the morning paper, a cup of coffee on the table before him, a cigarette dangling from his mouth. He grinned at her, stubbed out the cigarette, and jumped to his feet.

'Oh, it's good all right,' he said. 'In fact, it's great.'

She set her handbag down on the table and
shrugged out of her jacket. 'Well, how long are you
going to keep me in suspense? What is it?'

She hung up her jacket, then turned to face him.
His red hair was sticking up in all the wrong places,
as usual, his pale blue eyes alight with suppressed
excitement. And, instead of his usual shabby jeans
and sweat-shirt, he was wearing a suit!

For a moment, all she could do was goggle at
him. Granted, it was a decidedly disreputable suit—
a kind of faded green polyester that looked as
though it had been shoved in the bottom drawer of
his dresser and lain there for several years—but still
a suit. His brilliantly striped tie was badly knotted
and skewed sideways under his collar, and there was
a button missing from his shirt, but he'd obviously
made an effort to dress more formally than usual.

Rachel folded her arms across her chest and eyed
him narrowly. 'You must be celebrating something
pretty grand to get yourself all dolled up that way,'
she commented drily. 'Either that or someone has
died.'

He continued to beam on her the same smug,
fatuous grin. 'No one has died.'

'Well, for heaven's sake, Sam, will you please
put me out of my misery? What happened?'

'I got the money.'

She stared blankly at him. 'What money?'

'The money to keep the company from going
under.' He waved his hands in the air excitedly and
came to stand before her. 'You should know.
You've kept the books, after all, since I had to let

Martha go. Without a transfusion of cold hard cash, we'd have to close up shop in a month.'

As he spoke, Rachel's eyes gradually widened. 'Sam!' she exclaimed in a hushed voice. 'You mean to say that some poor unsuspecting bank has actually loaned you money on the strength of this?' She made a sweeping gesture that encompassed the shabby décor of the small room.

'Nope,' he replied. 'It's better than that. A chain of publishers wants to buy me out.'

She frowned as the implications of that statement sank in. 'But you don't want to lose the business, do you? Not after all the agony you've gone through trying to keep it going these past few years.'

'But that's the beauty of it!' he crowed. 'I won't lose the business. In exchange for a percentage of the profits——'

'Wait a minute,' she broke in, holding up a hand. 'What profits?'

'Will you please let me finish? You're always so damned practical, Rachel.'

'All right. Sorry. Go ahead.'

'It's quite simple,' he went on. 'The profits will come from expansion. They'll give me an infusion of capital so that we can broaden our base. You know the Puget Sound area is bursting with literary talent. We just haven't had the money to pay for the best writers, so all the really good ones have gone elsewhere. Now we can lure them back to us.'

'Well,' she said dubiously, 'it sounds promising. But, Sam, you shouldn't jump into anything without giving it careful thought, making a

thorough investigation. What's the name of the
company that's going to play Santa Claus for you?'

'Oh, I can't remember. Something with
Worldwide or Universal in it. But you can find out
all that yourself. The reason I got you down here
so early is that we're going to have breakfast with
their representative in...' He broke off to glance
at his watch. 'In fifteen minutes, to be exact. At
the Hilton, no less. And he's paying. Come on, we
can walk it in that time if we get going now.'

With a sigh, Rachel put her jacket back on and
they went outside, locking the office door behind
them. She knew that Sam's weak head for business
meant that she wouldn't get any more information
out of him. It was actually what made him such a
good publisher, with a canny eye for quality writing,
but it didn't do much for the financial end of it.

As they trudged up the steep hill towards the
Hilton, away from the busy harbour down below,
Sam chattered happily about his plans for expansion. They would hire a secretary, a recep-
tionist, and get Martha back to keep the books so
that Rachel could get on with her real work as
editor, the job she'd been hired to do in the first
place.

The company had been solvent then, but, with
the burgeoning number of new publishing firms
starting up all over the Puget Sound area, the com-
petition for good writers had become so fierce, and
Sam's business acumen so terrible, that he was only
hanging on now by a shoe-string. In fact, Rachel

herself had turned down more than one offer from other local companies, just out of loyalty to Sam.

As they approached the hotel at the top of the hill, she was out of breath from trying to keep up with his long strides and feeling distinctly dishevelled in her too heavy suit. She could feel the beads of perspiration on her face wreaking havoc with her careful make-up job, and knew her shoulder-length tawny hair was fast becoming limp and losing its set.

Inside the spacious, blessedly cool lobby she turned to him. 'Listen, I've got to make a stop in the powder-room and try to repair some of the damage.' She took off her jacket. 'Do you think this blouse looks dressy enough to impress your tycoon?'

Just then, glancing past Sam's shoulder, she saw a tall man ambling slowly across the lobby in their direction. She stood stock-still. Her heart simply stopped beating for a moment. Then it flipped over and started to thud noisily in her ears.

All she could do was stare. It couldn't be him! But it was. She'd recognise that walk anywhere, the slow, confident gait, the hands stuffed in trouser pockets, the lift of the broad shoulders, the perfect fit of the elegant dark suit, the crisp white shirt and muted tie. Then it dawned on her with a wave of sheer horror that he was heading directly for them.

It was too late to turn away. As he came closer she could see that he looked much the same as before—a little older, perhaps, the lines at the corners of his eyes a little deeper, a trace of grey

in the dark hair. But then it had been two years
since she'd seen him. She must have aged, too.
Instinctively, she raised a hand to her hair, regretting the fact that at his first sight of her in all
this time she'd look so bedraggled.

'Hello, Rachel,' he said when he reached them.
His voice was the same, too: low and quiet, but
with an authoritative ring to it.

'Hello, Stephen,' she replied. Then she turned to
Sam, who was staring at them open-mouthed. 'Is
this your representative, Sam?' she asked in a tight
voice.

He could only nod. 'You two know each other?'
he croaked out at last.

Stephen turned to him and smiled. 'You could
say that.' His dark grey eyes flicked at Rachel, then
back to Sam. 'In fact, we were married for five
years.'

Somehow Rachel got through the interminable
breakfast with at least a vestige of poise intact. At
least she didn't faint dead away or gibber unintel-
ligibly when she was expected to participate in the
discussion, which, to her intense relief, centred entirely on the business negotiations for Sam's
company.

Sam, of course, was bursting with curiosity about
the relationship between them. He managed to keep
it under wraps, however, until Stephen excused
himself and rose from his chair, signalling the end
of the meeting.

'Well, Sam,' he said, 'I think we have an agreement that will be mutually beneficial. Why don't you think it over? If you're satisfied, I'll have our lawyers draw up the contract.'

Sam jumped to his feet. 'I can tell you right now—it suits me down to the ground.' He glanced down at Rachel. 'What do you think, Rachel?' he asked.

'Let's talk about it later,' she replied firmly.

Stephen smiled. 'Wise woman,' he commented. 'You'd better listen to her, Sam. She always did have a level head. For business, that is.'

Rachel glanced up and gave him a sharp look. It was the first remotely personal remark he'd made all morning, and she had to wonder what he'd meant by it. The implication was that she wasn't quite so sensible or level-headed when it came to other matters. But his expression was bland, guileless. Only the steely eyes had that knowing look in them that she remembered so well, the look that hid what went on behind them, yet seemed able to penetrate to the core of her being.

'How long will you be staying in Seattle?' Sam was asking him now.

Stephen shrugged. 'I'm not sure. At the moment, my plans are up in the air. Let's see what develops in our negotiations—after you've had a chance to discuss it with Rachel. I'm in no hurry.'

Rachel suppressed the sharp retort that rose to her lips. Stephen Kincaid had never been unsure of his plans in his life, and she had to wonder what devious scheme he had cooked up now. Poor Sam!

She'd have to warn him. He was so eager to get the promised money that he'd sell his life away if he wasn't careful.

'Well,' Sam said, 'I'd like to show you the sights, if you're planning to stay indefinitely.'

'Oh, I know Seattle quite well,' Stephen replied. 'In fact, I was born here.' He looked down at Rachel. 'We both were.'

'I see,' Sam faltered. He looked from one to the other, obviously at a loss what to say.

Stephen turned back to him. 'I'll be in touch.' With that, he nodded, turned around, and strode away from the table.

When he was gone, Sam sank back down in his chair and gave Rachel a bewildered look. 'Well,' he said at last. 'That was quite a coincidence, wasn't it? I mean, I didn't even know you'd ever been married, much less to a man like Stephen Kincaid.'

'I guess I never thought it was worth discussing. It was a long time ago and I was very young. And very gullible. At any rate, whatever our former relationship was, it has no bearing on my life today or your negotiations with his company.'

He stared thoughtfully down at his empty plate for a moment, then turned to her with a broad grin. 'Well, at least that tells me one thing.'

'What's that?'

'You're not as set against marriage as I thought you were.' He laughed. 'All this time I thought you'd put me off because you were a confirmed spinster. Or should I say bachelorette? Now maybe there's hope for me.'

She shook her head vigorously. 'Sorry, Sam, it doesn't work that way. If anything, my marriage to Stephen Kincaid was what cured me of ever putting my neck in that noose again.' She rose abruptly to her feet. 'Let's get back to the office. We've got some talking to do about his proposition and can forget the personal aspect.'

But she soon discovered it wasn't going to be that easy. As the morning wore on, with Sam babbling happily away, making elaborate plans for their future expansion, Rachel found her mind wandering, only listening to him with half an ear.

Just why had Stephen shown up to bail Sam's company out of the doldrums at all? His position in the worldwide conglomerate he'd worked for for these past ten years was surely too exalted for such a minor task. Any junior executive could have done it just as well.

The last she'd heard of him, he'd been living in England, running the London office of the company. With the Atlantic Ocean between them, she'd felt safe. Now he'd come back into her life, and she had to wonder why.

Finally, at noon, after Sam had left for an early lunch date, she called her sister, Laura, and invited herself for a meal. She needed to get away from the office, needed to think over what had happened that morning, away from Sam and his blind euphoria, his enthusiastic plans for the future.

*   *   *

Laura's husband, John, was a prosperous attorney, and they lived with their four children in a large, imposing colonial house at the very top of Queen Anne Hill, with a sweeping hundred-and-eighty-degree view of Puget Sound, the snow-capped Olympic Mountains, the city and harbour spread out below, and, on a clear day, Mount Rainier.

The two sisters sat out in the back garden under the shade of an ancient weeping willow. It was Easter vacation, and all four children, ranging in age from seven to thirteen, were home, highly visible—and audible. Finally, Laura got them fed and settled with a game of Monopoly inside the house, and came back outside, mopping her brow.

'There,' she breathed, slumping down wearily at the table. 'That should keep them quiet for at least fifteen minutes and we can have our lunch in peace.' She gave Rachel a rueful glance. 'You don't know how lucky you are with your nice, peaceful life.'

'Oh, peace and quiet can get a little boring,' Rachel replied with a smile.

'Well, there's never a dull moment when you're raising kids!' Laura exclaimed with feeling. 'Besides, you love your work.'

'Yes, of course I do,' Rachel said hurriedly. 'But I'll have to admit I do sometimes regret not having children.'

Laura's eyebrows shot up. 'That's quite an admission, coming from you. Weren't you the one who kept putting it off?' Then she laughed. 'Besides, it's not too late. You're only twenty-eight. You still have lots of time.'

'Yes, but it takes two to produce children,' Rachel commented drily. 'And, in my view, to raise them. That's just not in the cards for me. I'm not complaining,' she added hastily when she saw the look on Laura's face. 'I made the decision, and I've learned to live with it.'

There was a small silence then, and Rachel could almost hear her sister biting her tongue. She knew quite well what Laura was thinking: *You had a husband who would have given you children, but you left him.* It was an old argument they'd been over many times in the past, until Rachel had finally put her foot down, simply refused to discuss it ever again.

But now everything had changed. She needed to talk to someone about Stephen's unexpected reappearance in her life, and Laura was the only one she could think of whom she could trust. If that meant reopening the old quarrel, she'd just have to risk it. Still, she hesitated, and sat there for several moments, staring down at the paper napkin she was slowly tearing to shreds in her lap.

'Actually,' she said at last, raising her head to face her sister, 'it's Stephen I wanted to talk to you about. He's shown up.'

Laura's mouth fell open. 'You mean here? In Seattle?'

Rachel nodded. 'Yes. It seems his company is interested in investing in Sam's publishing business, which, as you know, could use all the help it can get.'

'But why Stephen? Surely just about anyone could handle such a relatively minor matter?'

'Exactly what I thought.'

Laura leaned back in her chair and pursed her lips thoughtfully. 'So,' she said finally, 'why has he really come back? Is that what's bothering you?'

'Well, yes,' Rachel replied. 'I mean, I have this awful feeling that somehow he's here to make trouble for me.'

'Why on earth should he do that?'

Rachel shrugged. 'Well, the last time I saw him was not a very pleasant occasion. Remember, I left him.'

'How could I forget?' Laura remarked in a dry tone. 'You know quite well how I've always felt about that.' When she saw the warning look on Rachel's face, she held up a hand. 'All right, we won't go into that. But in any case, I can't see Stephen holding a grudge for two whole years.'

Rachel leaned forward in her chair and gave her sister an intense look. 'Laura, you can't imagine how badly his ego was wounded when I left him and got the divorce.'

'Well, yes, but still a man like Stephen wouldn't retaliate for that after all this time. I mean, sure, he's a hard man in many ways, a stubborn man, even somewhat ruthless, but there was nothing mean or petty about him. John always liked him.' She gave Rachel a long, hard look. 'And I can't help it. I still think you were a fool to let him go.'

Rachel sighed. 'Oh, Laura, I caught him with another woman. Are you saying I should have let it pass, just go on as though nothing had changed between us?'

'Well, of course things had to change after that. But there is a school of thought that considers divorce a worse crime than adultery.'

'Not in my book,' Rachel replied firmly. 'I was so much in love with him. And I thought he loved me. What we had was so perfect, and then . . .' Her voice broke and she looked away.

'Well, he *did* love you, you ninny! And no marriage is perfect. If you'd only waited, talked to him about it.'

Just then a sudden burst of childish screams emanated from the house. Laura threw up her hands and jumped to her feet. 'Hang on,' she called on her way to the back door. 'It sounds as though someone might be really hurt this time. Be right back.'

While she was gone, Rachel wiped her eyes and blew her nose, then leaned her head back on the chair. Silly to get so emotional over something long past, dead and gone. And she had to admit that what actually troubled her deep down was the fear that Laura was right, that she had acted too hastily in leaving Stephen the way she did.

And had their marriage been so perfect? She'd been at fault in many ways, too. She remembered the arguments they'd had long before that awful night of the party when she'd come across them . . . She squeezed her eyes shut as though to blot out the awful memory, but it wouldn't go away. She could still see them: Stephen and her best friend, locked in a passionate embrace on the bed—*her* bed—the woman half undressed, both of them a little drunk.

'No!' she cried aloud, banging her fist on the table. No matter what had gone wrong between them before that night, there was no excuse for what he'd done. She could never forgive him for that betrayal.

During the short bus ride back to town, no matter how hard she tried, Rachel couldn't get the things Laura had said off her mind. It had been a mistake to expect any help from that quarter. Laura meant well, but was so convinced the be-all and end-all for every woman was a solid marriage, a husband and family that she couldn't see any other way of life. Not to mention the fact that she'd always had a soft spot in her heart for Stephen and had always believed Rachel had been in the wrong.

All in all, it hadn't been the most fruitful conversation she'd ever had. In fact, it raised more questions than it resolved. She'd started out fretting over why Stephen had shown up after all these years. Now that the whole can of worms was open again, she was forced back into the past to re-examine the whole business all over again, something she'd imagined was settled once and for all.

By the time she stopped work for the day, the sky was overcast, rain threatened, and the breeze had grown decidedly chilly, and as she walked the short distance from the bus-stop to her house she was grateful for the woollen suit after all.

She'd stayed late at the office, trying to catch up on the pile of manuscripts she'd been avoiding for so long. For the past several weeks it had seemed hopeless to spend much time on them, since it looked as though there soon wouldn't be a company, and she had spent most of her time trying to juggle Sam's chaotic books and dealing with correspondence with his increasingly insistent creditors.

Now, however, with the prospect of new capital in the offing, she should be able to get back to her real job. Their publishing list consisted mostly of non-fiction works dealing with subjects of local interest, mainly environmental. Not exactly what she'd had in mind when she ventured upon a career in publishing, but the occasional lively writer with something interesting to say made it worthwhile.

The house she lived in was in the Laurelhurst section of Seattle, a quiet residential neigh-bourhood of older homes with wide streets and well-tended gardens. It was the first home she and Stephen had had after their marriage, and, as she let herself in the front door, it seemed suddenly to be full of him.

They'd only actually lived there for a year when his company had transferred him to their main office in New York, but since Stephen's new pos-ition meant more affluence they'd kept the house as a sort of home base for their trips back to Seattle, where they'd both grown up, renting it out occasionally.

After the divorce she'd moved back into it, grateful to have a home to go back to, but now, as she looked around the pleasant living-room, all she saw was the chair he used to sit in, the faded mark on the carpet where he'd spilled a cup of coffee, the clock on the mantel that had belonged to his dead parents.

Averting her eyes, she went quickly down the hall to the bedroom to change her clothes. At least she'd had the sense to get rid of their old bed—*the* bed, the one she'd found him sprawled out on that night with Margaret. Still, it was the same room, and as she stood there memories came flooding back, painful memories she'd been certain were long dead and buried.

But this was ridiculous! Was she going to let one encounter with him spoil her pleasure in the home she loved? It had been a shock, but she'd get over it. It had been bound to happen sooner or later. Before long he'd get his business taken care of and leave, and that would be the end of it.

After a shower and a light supper, she settled down in the living-room, deliberately choosing *his* chair, just to prove she could do it, and took out the manuscript she'd brought home with her to read. But she soon found she couldn't concentrate on it. No matter how hard she tried to avoid them, thoughts of Stephen kept popping into her mind.

She was just about to give up and turn on the television for distraction, when the telephone rang. It was Sam, sounding harried and out of breath.

'Sorry to bother you at home,' he said.

'That's all right. What's wrong? You sound as though you've been running.'

'Well, you might say that. Actually, that's the reason I'm calling. I just got a telephone summons from the new company to fly to New York first thing tomorrow morning.'

Rachel frowned. 'That's odd. I wonder why they want you to do that?'

'Oh, it seems they want to check me out personally before risking their money on me.'

'I can't imagine what they can learn from a personal interview that they couldn't find out from going over our books.'

'Listen, Rachel, at this point I'm not about to ask questions. That money means too much to me. Anyway, you'll have to hold down the fort by yourself while I'm gone.'

'All right. How long do you think you'll be away?'

'Who knows? As long as they want me. Well, I gotta run. I haven't even started to pack.'

After they'd hung up, Rachel stood by the telephone, frowning down at it. Why would the company want Sam to go to New York any more than they'd send a high-powered executive like Stephen to Seattle to check out the business? Something didn't ring quite true about the whole affair.

Sam had said the summons was by telephone from New York. Stephen, as far as she knew, was still in Seattle. So it couldn't have been his doing. Could it? Well, there was no reason why he couldn't have arranged it. But why?

Once again her suspicions about his sudden appearance back in her life burgeoned. But that made no sense either. If she imagined he was coming back to get revenge on her in some way after two years, she really was getting paranoid.

Rachel spent most of the next morning at the office continuing to plough her way through the stack of manuscripts on her desk. Sam had evidently taken the account books with him to New York, so there was no business to take care of. Even the creditors seemed to have got wind of Sam's new affluence and she didn't have to deal with one irate telephone call.

It was close to noon when she heard the front door open out in the reception room. It was almost time for lunch anyway, so she straightened out the pages she'd been reading, replaced them in their folder, and got up from her desk. When she opened the door to the reception room and saw Stephen standing there, the raindrops still glistening in his dark hair, she simply stopped short and stared.

'Hello, Rachel,' he said.

Her heart began to pound and her knees felt so weak that she was afraid they'd buckle under her. Why, after all this time, did he still have the power to affect her so profoundly? She drew in a deep breath, willing herself to be calm. Whatever it was he had on his mind, it was best to let him speak his piece, find out what he wanted, then deal with it as best she could.

'Sam's not here,' she said curtly.

'I know. It wasn't Sam I came to see.'

'I see.' She forced out a cool smile. 'Well, then, what can I do for you? I'm afraid Sam took the account books with him, but I'm pretty familiar with all the company's business affairs. Was there anything in particular you wanted to know?'

'How have you been, Rachel?' he asked.

'Well, fine. Just fine. And you?'

'Muddling along.'

'The last I heard you were in London. What brings you back to Seattle? Surely not just to handle this merger—or whatever you want to call it.'

He glanced around at the shabby office. They'd had to cancel the caretaking service weeks ago, and little puffs of dust bunnies were lying about on the floor. The elderly lampshade was crooked, the slats of the blinds at the one small window were covered with a greasy film, and in one corner near the ceiling an enormous black spider was busily spinning its web.

She stood there waiting, watching him as his grey eyes flicked over the deplorable sight. His face was expressionless, giving away nothing of his real feelings, but, from the arrogant tilt of his dark head, the set of his jaw, the casual stance, hands in his pockets, she knew exactly what he was thinking.

Finally, his gaze settled on her and he smiled. 'So,' he said, making a sweeping gesture with one hand. 'This is the great career you sacrificed so much for—yourself and everyone else.'

A sharp retort rose immediately to her lips, but she bit it back. She would be cool, distant, aloof, and she would not let him ruffle her feathers. He was apparently determined to goad her into anger, and she wouldn't give him the satisfaction.

'Well, I'll have to admit it's not much,' she said with a little laugh. 'But I enjoy the work. And besides, I wouldn't say the sacrifices were all that great.'

He raised one dark eyebrow. 'Oh, really?' Then he nodded. 'You don't call marriage, family, home much?'

Her cheeks burned. 'I don't know what you're talking about. You know quite well the reason our marriage failed, and it had nothing to do with my work.'

He took two long steps towards her, covering the distance between them so that he was now directly before her. He stood there for a moment without speaking, his eyes narrowed, his jaw working, a little pulse beating just below his ear. They were so close now that she could smell the familiar scent of his aftershave, the peculiarly *Stephen* scent that she recognised immediately even after all this time.

'And what reason was that?' he asked in a low voice. Although his tone was steady, Rachel knew him well enough to recognise the underlying throb of emotion in it.

'Oh, Stephen,' she said, turning away. 'What's the point of going into all that? We hashed it out to the point of nausea two years ago and got nowhere.'

'And you never listened to one word I had to say. You had your mind all made up about just what happened that night with Margaret, didn't you? Never mind the facts.'

'Stephen, I *saw* you!' she cried, eyes blazing, her fists clenched at her sides.

'You saw what you wanted to see,' he barked.

She'd done exactly what she'd sworn she wouldn't do—lost her temper, allowed her feelings to take over when what she needed was a cool head. With a supreme effort of will she steeled herself against the confusing welter of emotion that threatened to make her lose control altogether.

'Stephen,' she said in a tight voice, 'this is pointless. I don't see that anything is to be gained by discussing the past again. I *won't* discuss it.'

'All right,' he rejoined immediately. 'We won't, then.' She could see the tension draining out of his face, his shoulders relaxing. 'Now,' he went on, 'how about having lunch with me?'

'I don't think so.'

'Oh, come on. For old times' sake? After all, we grew up together, knew each other as children. Surely one lunch won't disturb your peace of mind? Or would it?'

She sighed deeply. His proximity was becoming more nerve-racking by the moment. She moved away from him, walking over to the window and peering out at the busy street. He didn't say anything, but she could hear his steady breathing behind her.

Finally she turned around to face him. 'All right, Stephen, you've made your point. Now, tell me. Why are you really here?'

He shrugged. 'Oh, lots of reasons. I wanted a change. And I've always thought of Seattle as my home, in a way. Then, when this business with Sam came up, I thought I might as well come back and oversee it personally.'

Rachel didn't think much of that rationale. She knew there had to be more to it than that. The Stephen Kincaid she knew never did anything without a good reason. In fact, she was more convinced than ever that he had masterminded the whole business with Sam himself. What she couldn't figure out was why.

She gave him a wary look. 'And that's all?'

He grinned broadly at her. 'Well, there is one more thing,' he added softly. 'Maybe I've decided to give you another chance.'

CHAPTER TWO

RACHEL stared at him, open-mouthed. 'You've got to be joking,' she finally managed to splutter.

'I never joke about important things,' Stephen assured her loftily. 'You should know that.'

'Well, then, you must be hooked on something. Of all the insane schemes you ever came up with, this has to be the limit.'

'I don't see why,' he said in a reasonable tone. 'Come on, admit it. There's still a spark there.'

'Oh, Stephen,' she said in a scathing tone. 'You're dreaming. That's all over, and you know it.'

'I don't see it that way.' He waved a hand in the air. 'It's really quite logical. If you hadn't cared so much, what you thought you saw between Margaret and me that night wouldn't have upset you so badly.'

'Upset me!' she cried. 'It was the worst betrayal one human being can commit against another! You spoiled everything.' She bit her tongue and gave him a cold stare. 'But I don't want to talk about that.'

'That's because you know you were wrong.'

'Think what you like. It's over, and there's no going back.'

'So you won't even talk about it reasonably, one human being to another?'

'No.' She turned from him and started back to her office. 'Now, I have work to do, so if you don't mind——'

'Well, that's too bad,' he broke in. 'I'd hate to disappoint Sam now that he's counting on our money to get back on his feet. Although, I must say,' he added with another swift glance around the shabby room, 'I'm not so sure it would be such a wise investment after all.'

She whirled around to face him. 'That's blackmail!'

'Not at all. Just sound business practice. I have sole discretion here as to whether it's a good investment to risk our money on, and from the looks of it I don't see that we'd have much to gain by bailing him out.'

She crossed her arms in front of her and glared at him. 'That's pretty low, Stephen,' she bit out. 'Even for you.'

'Oh, come on, Rachel. I didn't say I was going to do it. But if his one employee can only be obstructive and uncooperative, snapping at the hand that just might feed her...' He shrugged. 'What else can I do?'

She stood there biting her lip, thinking. 'All right,' she said at last. 'If it'll make you happy, I'll have lunch with you.'

He smiled. 'That's all I asked,' he said reasonably. 'Shall we go?'

They chose a popular seafood restaurant that was located at the end of one of the piers overlooking the harbour. It was slightly overcast, obscuring the mountains off in the distance, but it was still quite pleasant to sit by the window watching the ferries crossing the Sound to the neighbouring islands, the busy cargo ships loading and unloading at the dock.

In spite of her lingering irritation at his high-handed attitude, Rachel found it rather enjoyable to be squired by a man like Stephen once again. There was something about his confident manner that made head waiters fawn on him, and he somehow always ended up with the best table, even in the most crowded restaurants.

Nor had it escaped her that he still had the power to turn the head of virtually every other woman in the place when the waiter conducted them to their table. It had been a long time since she'd been out with a man that attractive.

After they'd ordered, he gazed pensively out of the window at the busy harbour for a while, then settled back in his chair and smiled at her. 'Ah, it's good to be back in Seattle. I'd forgotten what a beautiful city it is. In spite of all the new construction.'

'Is this your first trip back, then?' she asked.

He nodded. 'Yes. I've hardly been in the States at all since I was posted in London. Now I'm ready to come home for good.'

She goggled at him, suddenly alert to the implications of that statement. 'You don't mean to live here, in Seattle?'

'I haven't decided. I kept my apartment in New York, or rather the company kept it for me, but somehow I don't relish the thought of living in that jungle on a permanent basis.' He shrugged. 'I'll have to see what happens before I make up my mind.'

Their food arrived just then, and the subject was dropped. As they chatted over lunch about old friends they'd had in common, their past experiences, Rachel's uneasiness gradually began to leave her. After all, wasn't it the civilised thing to do these days, to be on friendly terms with one's ex-spouse? She knew she'd wounded his ego badly by leaving him, but he didn't seem to be after revenge, as she'd first feared. Maybe they could even be friends. At least, not enemies.

'So,' he said over coffee, 'tell me about what you've been doing these past few years. I mean in your personal life. For instance, have you and your redheaded boss got something hot and heavy going between you?'

She almost choked on her coffee. 'Lord, no!' she exclaimed, wiping her mouth. 'It's strictly business between us.' She gave him a wary glance. 'How about you? I suppose you've run the gamut of most of the desirable women in the world by now.'

He threw back his head and laughed. 'You flatter me,' he said at last. 'But then you always did have an exaggerated view of my interest in women. To answer your question, though, I'll have to admit I've done my share of experimenting, as I'm sure you have, but that's about all.'

'Then you haven't considered marrying again?' she commented cautiously.

He eyed her with something like horror. 'God, no!' he said with feeling. 'In my view, everyone deserves one chance at it. If that doesn't work you've got to consider the possibility that you're not cut out for it at all.'

'Oh, come on, Stephen. Are you saying that if one marriage fails, that's the end of it; you never get a second chance?'

'Well, I haven't noticed that changing partners solves very much. If you can't make it with your first choice, chances are you won't with the second or third, either.'

'A lot of people would disagree with that theory.'

'Obviously,' he commented drily. 'All you have to do is take a look at the sky-rocketing divorce rate, especially for second tries.' He drained his coffee. 'All right,' he said. 'Now that we've brought each other up to date and found the coast is clear on both sides, let's talk about us.'

'There is no "us" any more, Stephen,' she said in a tight voice. 'Remember?'

'Listen, we're both free. We're old friends. You're still a damned attractive woman. There's no reason why we shouldn't get some pleasure from each other's company. The world is getting smaller all the time, and since my firm is venturing into publishing now I could probably help you in your career.'

Her face closed down and she gave him a wary look. 'I don't know what you're after, Stephen, but whatever we had together is over, finished. I agree that as mature adults we should be able to meet on a friendly basis, especially if we're going to live in the same town, be involved in business together. But that's as far as it can ever go.'

'I don't see why,' he said in a reasonable tone. 'As I said, you're still an attractive woman.' He reached across the table and put his hand over hers. 'We used to have some good times together, Rachel. We could again.'

'No,' she stated flatly. 'It's not possible.'

'Come on, Rachel, don't be like that.' The grey eyes glinted at her and his hand tightened on hers. 'After all,' he said in a lower, more confidential tone, 'in spite of our past differences, you'll have to admit that bed was one place we never had any problem.'

Her face went up in flame at the reminder, and for one brief moment she was even tempted. He was still attracted to her, obviously, and she had to admit that, as far as sheer masculine appeal went, he'd be hard to beat. In the two years they'd been divorced, she hadn't met one man who remotely compared with him in looks, personality or blatant physical attraction.

And he was right: their lovemaking had been near perfect. But that was the main reason his betrayal had hurt so terribly, and she immediately hardened her heart against him. To see the man she'd given herself to so unreservedly in bed with another woman had simply meant the end of everything. Her world had come crashing down around her ears that night, and now here he was, proposing to pick up right where they'd left off.

'That's not possible, Stephen, and you know it,' she said at last in a tone of finality. She drew her hand away and reached for her handbag. 'Now, I really should get back to the office. Since you so conveniently got Sam out of the picture, I have to run things alone.'

He gave her one of his most maddeningly arrogant smiles. 'Did I do that?' Then he sobered. 'Listen, Rachel, I'm not going to beg, but I think you owe it to me at least to consider my proposal.'

She stared at him, speechless. 'Owe it to you, Stephen?' she asked in a scathing tone. 'I don't understand how you can even suggest such a thing. If you will recall, I caught you in bed with my best friend.'

His face hardened, and he leaned across the table until his face was only inches away from hers. 'For the record, Rachel, once and for all, I did *not* go to bed with Margaret!'

'Close enough to it not to make any difference,' she remarked bitterly.

'I'm not going to explain about that again, Rachel,' he said in a warning tone. 'I tried to tell you at the time what really happened—exactly nothing, as a matter of fact—but you wouldn't listen then, and I have no reason to believe you'd listen now.'

'Right,' she said, rising to her feet. 'And so we really have nothing to talk about, do we? Now, I'm going back to the office.'

She sailed out of the restaurant, head held high, without a backward glance to see if he was following her. It wasn't until she was out on the street that she sneaked a glance behind her. He was nowhere in sight. Breathing a sigh of relief, she headed back the few blocks to the office, her face still burning, her heart still pounding.

He'd *almost* talked her into something she knew she'd be sorry for. What was there about the man that made his crazy rationale so plausible? Imagine him coming back here after all this time, calmly assuming she'd be delighted to take up right where they'd left off, just as though they were still married, and hop back into bed with him! And, what was worse, she'd been perilously close to doing it!

She'd forgotten Stephen once, and she could do it again.

But she soon found it wasn't going to be that easy. The seed he'd planted seemed to be spreading its roots and sprouting so vigorously that by the time she got home that night it was all she could think about.

She wandered aimlessly about the house, which somehow now seemed so empty, yet, as her gaze fell on each reminder of him, so full of Stephen. With his sudden eruption into her life again, the life she'd thought was so satisfying now began to look barren and pointless. They'd been so happy here, so much in love, their future so bright and full of promise.

On an impulse she went to the sideboard in the dining-room and opened the bottom drawer, where, for some sentimental reason, she'd kept the album of their wedding photographs. She hadn't even looked at them in the past two years, ever since the divorce, but now she felt oddly impelled to glance through it once again.

She took the album out of the drawer and carried it into the living-room where, without thinking, she sat down in *his* chair by the fireplace and set it down on the table in front of her. She stared down at it for several long seconds, almost as though she was afraid to open it. It was all coming back to her now—the happiest day of her life.

Then, slowly, she opened the cover.

The very first picture was the one that had always been her favourite, and as she gazed down at it the old familiar ache pierced her heart. It was of the two of them alone. She was heading up the staircase of her parents' home to her old bedroom to change out of her wedding dress into her going-away suit, leaning over the banister looking down at him, he gazing up at her.

Stephen looked so handsome in the formal tails, tall and strong, his dark hair gleaming, white teeth flashing as he smiled up at her. And everyone had said she'd been a beautiful bride. The white satin dress had fit her to perfection, the gauzy veil like a halo around her tawny head. It was actually a candid shot, unposed, and the camera had caught the expressions on their faces perfectly—expressions of total love, trust, self-giving.

She thought about their blissful honeymoon in the Bahamas, their wedding night, how gentle and tender he'd been with her inexperience, how they'd swum nude one night and made love on the deserted beach, of his tall, hard body lying next to hers, the way he would reach out for her first thing every morning.

Recalling that total love and trust, the ache in her heart became almost more than she could bear, and hot tears stung behind her eyes. She knew then that, in spite of his betrayal, in spite of her best efforts to forget, in her heart she still loved him. She always would. Perhaps, she thought, she was one of those women who needed to be married, to give herself to one man totally and for life.

As the tears threatened to spill over, she gave herself a little shake and quickly turned the page to the next photograph. It was of the entire wedding party, just as they'd been six years ago. Her parents had been alive then, before the car crash that had so tragically killed them both not long afterwards, and there they all were, her father looking uncomfortable in his formal garb, her mother beaming, Laura as matron of honour.

And there, at the end of the line, was Margaret Fulton, one of the four bridesmaids—her best friend, and the one who had betrayed her. She had been the beauty of their crowd, with long silky black hair, wide green eyes, a perfect figure, tall and slim, and, as Rachel could see now, with an extremely sensual look about her, a look that exuded sexual promise.

Rachel slammed the book shut. She hadn't spoken to Margaret or even seen her for two years.

After that night, she'd cut her out of her life completely, along with Stephen. The two of them, she thought, as she thrust the book back in its drawer, the two people she'd loved and trusted most in the world, had betrayed her, and she would never forgive them.

After crying herself to sleep that night—actually the first real tears she'd shed since the divorce—she dreamed constantly. Each dream contained an image of Stephen—not the man who had betrayed her, but the man she'd loved so deeply—and she awoke the next morning with a lingering impression of him in her mind, so vivid that when she opened her eyes she half expected to see his dark head lying on the pillow next to her, just as it used to.

However, in spite of the pain those memories had reawakened, perhaps because of it, going over those wedding photographs had actually acted as a sort of catharsis for her. It was as though the tears she'd shed last night had washed away much of the bitterness she'd kept alive, and what remained, oddly, was only the powerful attraction she'd once felt for him.

Was it possible there was a chance they could give it another try? He certainly seemed eager to do so. It couldn't hurt anything to go out with him once if he asked her.

She sat up in bed, stretched widely, and glanced out of the bedroom window at the pouring rain. It was Saturday, and although there was plenty to do at the office she might as well give herself a day off, perhaps make some headway in the stack of manuscripts she'd brought home with her if she felt like it.

With that decision made, there was no need to get up just yet. It wasn't quite eight o'clock, and she'd spent a restless night with all that dreaming. She flopped over on her stomach and was just drifting off to sleep again when the telephone beside her bed rang. Stephen, she thought, as she reached out and snatched it up.

'Hello.'

'Hi, Rachel. It's me.'

'Oh, hello, Sam.'

'Well, try to contain your enthusiasm,' he remarked drily.

She laughed. 'I'm sorry, Sam. I'm still in bed, half asleep. Why are you calling so early?'

'Early! It's eleven o'clock, my girl.'

'Not here, it isn't. Remember, New York is three hours ahead of the West Coast.'

'Oops. Sorry, Rachel. I forgot.'

'Oh, that's OK. It's time I was getting up, anyway. So, why are you calling?'

'I just wanted to let you know I'm flying back tomorrow and will be in the office bright and early Monday morning.'

'So, how did it go? Any progress on the merger?'

'Yep. All signed, sealed and delivered. Overton Publishing is now a subsidiary of a huge conglomerate that for some reason seems anxious to pour money into it.'

'Well, that's great,' she said dubiously. 'What are their conditions?'

'No conditions. No strings. They seem to think we could work into a little gold mine for them, with enough capital investment to get us on our feet again. Which is only peanuts to them, anyway.'

'Well, I hope you're right, Sam. It still sounds a little fishy to me. I wish you'd consulted a lawyer before you signed anything.'

'Oh, Rachel, come on. You're such a killjoy. A born pessimist.'

'I am not,' she rejoined tartly. 'I'm just cautious—a quality, I might add, that you could use a little more of. But it's your company, Sam, and you have every right to do whatever you want with it. So long as you're happy, I'm happy for you.'

There was total silence on the line then, and Rachel began to think they'd been cut off. Either that, or she'd hurt Sam's feelings so badly that he'd hung up on her. She was just about to replace the receiver to clear the line so he could call her back, when he spoke again, this time in a more subdued tone.

'There is one stipulation,' he said. 'But nothing I can't live with,' he added hastily.

'What stipulation?'

'Well, only that Stephen Kincaid acts as a kind of overseer. I mean,' he rushed on, 'no real veto power, and they promised no interference with my policies, but he will be a presence in the operation. A sort of silent partner.'

'I see,' she said in a tight voice.

'I hope you can handle that, Rachel. I mean, considering your past—well, you know.'

'Yes, I know. Well, we'll just have to wait and see how it works out, won't we?'

'Don't be mad at me, Rachel. I didn't have any choice. It was either accept that one condition or lose the contract. And since that would mean folding up the business anyway, I figured it was worth a try. I don't want to lose you, Rachel, but if the company goes bust I wouldn't have a job to offer you anyway.'

'Of course, Sam,' she assured him. 'I understand. And so long as Stephen actually does remain "silent" I see no problem.'

What she didn't say was that in no circumstances could she envisage Stephen Kincaid as a passive bystander in any enterprise whatsoever. Nor could she blame Sam for taking such a step. He was right. He really did have nothing to lose, and it could work out for him, even with Stephen's ominous presence hovering in the background.

What remained to be seen was how it would work out for her.

The next day was Sunday, and, as usual, Rachel spent the afternoon at her sister's. It was another unseasonably fine day, and John had taken the children to the zoo.

'So,' Laura said when they had settled themselves at the kitchen table over a cup of tea, 'how are things progressing with Stephen?'

Rachel stared at her, then carefully set her cup down on the table. 'They're not,' she replied shortly. 'What in the world gave you the idea that there was anything to progress?'

Laura shrugged. 'Well, he manoeuvred his way back to Seattle for only one reason that I can see.'

'Oh? And what's that?'

'Why, to patch things up with you, of course.'

'Oh, Laura, don't be silly. He came back here because this is his home.'

'And that's why you had lunch with him the other day?'

'How did you know about that?'

Laura laughed. 'You know, dear, in spite of the tremendous growth in the area in the past ten years, Seattle is still basically a small town, especially for those of us who grew up here. Let's just say the grapevine is as effective as ever.'

Rachel gave an exasperated sigh. 'All right. I had lunch with him. I had to. He virtually threatened to withdraw his firm's support from Sam's company if I didn't.'

Laura nodded owlishly. 'Oh, I see. And that's the only reason you went, I take it.'

Rachel had to smile. 'All right, you win. I'll have to admit I was a little curious.'

'Just curious?'

'Of course. What else?'

Laura leaned across the table and fixed her sister with a long, piercing look. 'You want to know what I think?'

'Not really, but I'm sure you're going to tell me anyway.'

'I think you're still in love with him.' Rachel opened her mouth to object to that little bit of wisdom, but Laura held up a hand to stop her. 'Now, you just listen to me. He obviously wants you back. And no matter how much you deny it, I'm convinced you want him too. I know you, Rachel. You're the kind of woman who loves once and that's it. It's forever or nothing with you. And for the past two years I've watched you pining away, trying to make up for what you lost—what you threw away!—out of that silly job——'

But now Rachel had had enough. 'Now you're going too far,' she said, cutting off the end of Laura's sentence, and glaring at her. 'Listen to me——'

But Laura managed to out-glare her. 'No!' she broke in. 'You listen to me, for a change. I'm going to have my say at last, whether you like it or not. Now, as I said, I think you're still in love with Stephen. And he's obviously still in love with you, wants you back. He says nothing happened that night with Margaret Fulton. So why not just take him on faith? What have you got to lose?'

When she heard the note of genuine concern in her sister's voice, Rachel's anger dissipated. She knew quite well that Laura's only interest in the matter was her happiness.

'Now I suppose you're mad at me,' Laura said grimly.

Rachel had to smile. 'No. I'm not mad. I know you're only thinking of me, what you believe is best for me. I just don't think you realise...'

Just then the front door was flung open and high-pitched childish voices erupted into the quiet house, interspersed with John's deeper and totally ineffectual remonstrances.

'Ah, the vandals have returned,' Laura said, rolling her eyes and sighing deeply. 'But please, Rachel, think about what I've said. You'll always be sorry if you don't give it one more try.'

In the days that followed, that was virtually all Rachel could think about. In spite of her strenuously voiced objections to her sister's interference, what she had said made a lot of sense. And, at bottom, she had to admit that she'd been right about the futility of trying to replace love with a job. Maybe—just maybe—there might be a second chance for them.

The trouble was that he didn't give her that chance. As the days passed with no word from him, she had to conclude that he'd taken her at her word. After all, she'd now rejected him twice, and even a man like Stephen, with his powerful ego, would have trouble dealing with that. In the end, she told herself, it was probably for the best.

Sam had returned to the office on Monday, full of his plans for the future. She'd listened to him as he soared into totally unrealistic flights of fancy, but this time without her usual attempts to bring him back to earth. Her heart just wasn't in it.

To make matters worse, on Friday her car died, and she was faced with the long-delayed decision to have the transmission replaced. That not only meant a whopping repair bill, but also that she'd have to do without a car for several days.

She called Laura on Friday night to tell her she wouldn't be able to make it for her usual Sunday visit.

'So,' she ended her explanation, 'since I'll be without a car until Tuesday, at the earliest, I guess I'll be house-bound until then.'

'Oh, no!' Laura wailed. 'You've got to come. I was counting on it. John's parents have the kids for the weekend, and I was planning to try out a new recipe on you.'

Rachel smiled to herself. Laura thought of herself as a budding gourmet cook, and she hadn't tried one new concoction yet that hadn't turned out to be a disaster. Yet she wouldn't give up, and Rachel had been the victim of one failure after another, along with the mild-mannered, long-suffering John.

'I'll be sorry to miss that,' she lied.

'I know what,' Laura said in a brighter tone. 'John can come and pick you up and take you home. It's not that far, and he won't mind.'

Rachel dredged up every objection to that scheme she could think of, but Laura successfully countered every one of them, so that in the end she agreed to the plan. She knew John really wouldn't mind, and it wouldn't hurt her to try another spectacular flop from Laura's culinary efforts. So far she hadn't managed to actually poison her family, and who knew? This time she might come up with something edible.

Rachel was very fond of her brother-in-law, John. He was a tall, balding, mild-mannered man, who— she often wondered why—seemed to dote on his wife and family. A successful lawyer, he also managed to provide them with a distinctly comfortable lifestyle.

'So,' she said in the car on the way, 'what is Laura planning to feed us this time? I hope it's more edible than that last disaster. Sweetbreads, wasn't it?'

John laughed, a deep rumble. 'Something like that.' He sighed. 'I keep telling her I'm basically a meat and potatoes man, but she insists that cooking is a creative outlet for her, and I always end up feeling like some kind of insensitive brute whenever I complain.'

'Well, there's always Alka-Seltzer,' Rachel said philosophically. 'And she hasn't killed us yet.'

It was raining again, and, since every parking space in front of their house was full, John let her out at the kerb while he took the car around the corner to the garage in the back alleyway.

She ran up the front path, covering her head with her handbag for protection, and when she reached the front door Laura was there waiting for her.

'Where's John?' she asked, peering behind Rachel.

'He went to put the car in the garage,' she replied, brushing off her raincoat and stepping inside. There was an odd aroma in the air, and she sniffed suspiciously. 'Something smells—interesting,' she remarked.

'Well, it's a surprise,' Laura said firmly. 'I'm not going to tell you what it is.'

Probably just as well, Rachel thought as she shed her coat. 'I'll just put my things in the bedroom, all right?'

She started down the hall towards the back of the house, but when she reached the entrance to the large living-room the familiar tall figure of Stephen suddenly appeared, lounging casually against the archway, drink in hand. She stopped short, staring.

'Hello, Rachel,' he said.

She swivelled around to glare at Laura, but all she could see was her sister's aproned figure scurrying away towards the kitchen. She turned slowly back to face him.

'What are you doing here?' she demanded.

He raised one dark eyebrow and grinned at her. 'Why, I was invited, of course.'

Just then John came inside. He stopped for a moment, gazing at the little tableau spread before him with troubled eyes and glancing uncomfortably from one to the other. Then he, too, hurried past them down the hall.

'Better go see if Laura needs any help,' he muttered.

When he was gone, Rachel looked at Stephen again. What she wanted to do was kill her sister for manoeuvring her into this awkward situation, but since that really wasn't in the cards she'd just have to make the best of it.

CHAPTER THREE

THERE was one thing to be said about that evening: at least Rachel's acute discomfiture over Stephen's presence at the table did manage to deflect her attention from Laura's latest attempt at *haute cuisine*. She didn't even have to make her usual valiant effort to ignore what it was she was putting into her mouth, chewing, swallowing. It all tasted like cardboard anyway.

Thankfully, John and Stephen carried the burden of conversation, chatting away about sports, politics, business like the old friends they were, in typical masculine solidarity, and completely ignoring the two women. Throughout the meal Laura kept giving her nervous glances, obviously anxious to determine just how angry she was at the underhanded trick she'd played on her, but Rachel studiously ignored her sister's eyes. She'd have it out with her later.

However, in spite of her unease, there were moments when Rachel had the odd sensation that time had stopped two years ago, and the four of them were having Sunday dinner together, just as they used to. It was almost as though an invisible string still tied them together, even after all this time, and although she couldn't utter a word she was intensely aware of the man sitting across from her, the way he held his head slightly to one side while he listened to John, the sound of his voice, deep and confident, with the same old undercurrent of humour in it, and especially his sheer physical presence, his good looks, which, if anything, had improved with maturity.

This man had belonged to her once, and she had belonged to him. They had lived together for four years, planned their future together, lain in each other's arms at night. All those things were not as easily forgotten as she'd imagined.

Laura tried occasionally to enter the conversation, offering an opinion on the topic under discussion. John would turn to her then, give her an indulgent smile, pretend to listen attentively, then, as soon as he decently could, turn back to Stephen.

All Rachel wanted was to get out of there, and, as soon as they'd finished a dessert that was coloured a bright green, with a spongy texture and an odd flavour she couldn't for the life of her identify, she saw her chance when Laura rose from her chair and beamed down at them.

'Coffee, anyone?' she asked brightly.

Rachel jumped to her feet. 'Not for me, thanks. In fact, if you don't mind, I think I'll be on my way.'

'You can't go!' Laura spluttered, turning on her.

Ignoring her sister's frantic eye signals, Rachel turned quickly to her brother-in-law, who was slowly getting to his feet. 'No, John, please don't bother. I'll call a taxi.'

Stephen glanced up and gave her a direct look for the first time since they'd sat down at the table. 'That won't be necessary,' he said. 'I'll drive you home.'

'No, thank you,' she said quickly. 'I can just as easily—— '

'Nonsense,' he broke in. 'I'll take you.' He wiped his mouth with his napkin and laid it down beside his plate, then stood up and smiled at his hostess. 'Thanks for the fine meal, Laura.'

'Oh, not at all,' Laura gushed. 'And thank you for dropping Rachel off. John still has to go pick up the children and it'll save him a lot of time.'

Rachel glared at her sister, who now seemed as anxious to get rid of her as she had been to keep her a moment ago. But she knew it was hopeless. She was caught, and unless she wanted to create a scene she'd just have to go through with it.

'Sorry to leave so early,' Stephen was saying now to John, 'but I just flew in from New York this morning and have a long day tomorrow.'

Rachel swivelled her head around and gave him a sharp look. So that's where he'd been! That's why he hadn't called her! All of a sudden it didn't seem such a bad plan for him to drive her home after all. What she wanted most of all was to get out from under the watchful eye of her sister.

'I'll just go get my things,' she said.

Neither of them had much to say on the way home. Rachel sat stiffly beside him, her hands clasped tightly around her handbag, her mind a whirl, still a little stunned at the fact that she was sitting in a car beside her husband again. In one way, it seemed perfectly natural, but in another rather eerie. And it hadn't escaped her that she'd automatically still referred to him mentally as her husband.

Stephen drove as he always had, one elbow propped against the window-sill, both hands resting lightly on the wheel, and his attention firmly concentrated on the traffic, especially the dreadful snarl at the entrance to the motorway.

'I see Seattle drivers haven't improved much since I've been away,' he commented as he deftly merged into the flow of automobiles racing north.

She laughed. 'No. In fact, I've given up using the inter-state altogether. I find I get there just as fast on the side-roads, especially during the rush-hours.'

'Good idea,' he said, and took the next exit. 'Still living in the same place, I take it,' he said casually after a short silence.

It wasn't quite a question. She knew instantly that he was well aware of exactly where she lived, and she had to wonder how. Had he been keeping track of her? Somehow, instead of irritating her the way it probably should, this realisation filled her with a warm glow.

He pulled up in front of her house, set the hand-brake, switched off the ignition, then sat there for a few moments, his hands still lying on the steering-wheel. Rachel stole a quick sideways glance at him, and in the dim glow of the street-light on the corner she could see that, although he was not quite frowning, his expression was decidedly pensive.

She cleared her throat. 'Well, thanks for the lift. I'd better...'

But by then he'd already opened his door, stepped out of the car, and was on his way around the front to her side. She swiftly opened her own door and got out on to the pavement before he could reach her. When he did, they stood there for a few moments without speaking.

Then he smiled down at her. 'I could use a cup of coffee.'

For only a fraction of a second she hesitated. 'All right,' she said slowly. 'I think I can manage that.'

When they were inside the house, her sense of *déjà vu* grew much stronger. It was almost as if he'd never been gone. As always, when he was in it, he seemed to fill the house with his presence, to belong there.

She slipped out of her raincoat and hung it up in the hall cupboard, then turned back to him. But he had already gone on ahead, and when she went into the living-room she saw that he had switched on the lamp beside the couch and was standing in the middle of the room, his slightly hooded eyes flicking around it, his face expressionless.

Then he turned to her. 'You haven't changed much,' he said quietly. 'I see you've even kept my chair in the old spot.'

'It's a comfortable chair,' she said evenly.

'I always found it so.'

The stilted conversation was beginning to get on her nerves. All of a sudden she saw him as a complete stranger. What was she thinking of to invite this man into her house, her sanctuary, the one place in the world where she could really feel safe, be herself?

'Well, sit down,' she said at last in a stiff voice. 'I'll just go and make the coffee. I'm afraid it'll have to be instant.'

He only nodded in reply, and as she turned to leave she saw that he'd already started to saunter around the room, his hands in his trouser pockets, perfectly at ease, examining each object he came to as though to see if he recognised it.

He seemed relaxed enough, she thought irritatedly as she stalked down the hall to the kitchen. When she reached it, she closed the door, then leaned back against it with her eyes closed tight, listening to her heart pounding in her ears.

'This is stupid!' she muttered aloud at last, and pushed herself away.

She filled the kettle at the sink, set it on the stove, and reached into the cupboard for the jar of coffee, two mugs. He'd never used cream or sugar, and she assumed he still didn't. She spooned coffee into the mugs, then stood by the stove waiting for the kettle to boil, still pondering what in the world had made her agree to his coming inside the house. *Her* house, now.

So absorbed was she in her thoughts that she didn't hear the door open or realise he'd come inside until he spoke her name in a low voice, directly behind her.

She jumped slightly, then tensed. 'Yes?' she replied guardedly.

'I don't really want any coffee.' His hand came to rest on her shoulder. 'I think you know what I really want.'

She couldn't speak, could scarcely breathe, could only stand there, waiting. The hand on her shoulder moved to the back of her neck, lifted the heavy fall of tawny hair, his fingers running through the silken strands.

'I've always loved your hair,' he murmured. 'I'm glad you still wear it the same way. It suits you.'

'Stephen,' she said in a choking voice. 'Stop. Please stop.' She still couldn't turn around to look at him, didn't trust herself, didn't want him to see her face.

He bent his head now, moving her hair aside, and placed his mouth on the skin at the nape of her neck. A shiver ran through her at the touch of his lips. Mindlessly, she closed her eyes and allowed her body to sink back against him.

Immediately, as though he'd only been waiting for that one sign of acquiescence, his arms came around her, pressing her all along the hard length of his body. He buried his mouth in her hair, close to her ear, his breath coming warm and soft.

'I still want you, Rachel,' he breathed. 'You know that.'

She twisted her head around to look up at him, a protest already formed on her lips, but before she could get it out his open mouth had come down hard on hers. Even the taste of him was so familiar that she was transported back in time again. Her lips parted under his, and as his tongue flicked inside her mouth the hand at her waist moved upward to cup her breast.

Just then the kettle began to whistle, and the shrill, piercing sound that filled the room shattered the spell he'd cast over her and brought her abruptly to her senses. She tore herself out of his arms and reached out to lift the kettle from the burner and switch it off.

'Since you don't want any coffee,' she said, without turning around, 'perhaps you'd better go now.'

For a moment he didn't say anything. From behind her she could hear his laboured breathing as he struggled for control. Knowing she still had this power over him gave her a heady sense of elation, but the interruption had come just in time. She'd been on the verge of falling into a dangerous situation she'd sworn never to risk again.

'Rachel,' he rasped at last. 'Look at me.'

Slowly, she turned around to face him. 'What is it?'

'Why are you playing these games with me?' His face was set, his voice harsh.

'It's not a game, Stephen,' she said evenly. 'I don't know what you think gives you the right to come barging back into my life after two years of silence, but I'm not having any.'

'Two years of silence!' he bit out angrily. '*You* divorced *me*, if you will recall.'

She waved a weary hand in the air. 'Oh, what difference does it make now? We can't turn back the clock. It's too late. I have a new life. So do you.'

He took a step towards her, and although his jaw was still set, a little pulse still throbbing there, when he spoke his voice was soft. 'You still want me, Rachel. Don't deny it. You can't hide what you felt just now when I held you in my arms.'

Flushing deeply at the reminder, she deliberately hardened her heart against him and raised her chin. 'All right,' she said. 'I won't deny it. But it doesn't matter,' she added swiftly. 'I just can't forget, Stephen, what you did to me, what I saw that night. There's no way I can make you understand how completely it spoiled my feelings for you.'

He threw up his hands in a gesture of baffled disgust. 'How many times do I have to tell you?' he shouted. '*Nothing* happened!'

'Nothing?' she asked quietly.

A light flush passed over his face and he shrugged. 'Well, virtually nothing. We were celebrating my promotion that night, if you recall. I had more than I needed to drink, Margaret was there, and I just lost my head for a minute. But,' he added hastily, 'what you saw was as far as it went. I swear it. And it meant absolutely nothing.'

'Well, that was enough as far as I was concerned,' she retorted. 'I still have nightmares about it, still see the two of you together, on the bed . . .'

She broke off and turned away. 'Please, Stephen,' she said brokenly. 'Please just go now.'

For a time there was no sound at all in the room except the ticking of the clock on the counter, the rain pattering against the window. Then she heard his footsteps moving away from her. She perked up her ears and stood there, every muscle tense, until she heard the front door open and close.

It wasn't until she heard the car start up out in front and drive away that she slumped against the counter, put her head down, and let the tears come.

The next morning, as usual, she rode the crowded bus into the office, bright and early, but exhausted after a sleepless night, and still jumpy from the tense scene with Stephen. But even aside from that, what concerned her now was the prospect of having to work with him—or *for* him, more likely. Would he take his failure with her out on Sam?

No, that wasn't like Stephen, to take his revenge on her by harming an innocent third party. And, after all, what could he do to her, but fire her? And that wouldn't be the end of the world. What really bothered her was having to face him. He could even be there at the office now.

But when she stepped inside there was only Sam, sprawled out on the one chair in the tiny reception room, frowning down at a thick, forbiddingly legal-looking document.

'Ah, Rachel,' he said, brightening and leaping to his feet. 'I need your cool business head.' He shoved the document at her. 'Will you please try to plough your way through this maze of gobbledegook and tell me what I've signed?'

'Oh, Sam,' she said with a sigh. 'I thought you told me you were satisfied with it.'

He scratched his red head and wrinkled his brow. 'Well, I was at the time. I guess I was so relieved at getting out from under the gun financially, and what they told me seemed so plausible...' He shrugged helplessly.

She glanced down at the contract in her hand, then riffled briefly through the pages. It was at least thirty pages thick, much of it in fine print. She sighed again and gave Sam a dirty look.

'What you need is a good lawyer. Why don't I ask John to take a look at it?'

Sam brightened. 'Would you do that?'

She nodded. 'Of course.'

'Well, that's all right, then. But you can give it a quick once-over before he comes, can't you? Just so one of us will have some idea what we're talking about at the meeting.'

She gave him a puzzled look. 'Before who comes? What meeting?'

'Oh, didn't I tell you?' he asked innocently. 'Why, Stephen Kincaid, of course. I thought I already mentioned it.'

'No,' she stated firmly. 'You didn't.'

'Well, as you know, he's to be the silent partner, and he set up a meeting here for nine-thirty.'

'If he's so silent, why does he need a meeting?'

Sam rolled his eyes. 'How am I supposed to know? Come on, Rachel. Be a sport. Just look through it before he comes and see if you find any snags I should know about.'

Rachel set her handbag and the contract down on the chair, then removed her coat and hung it up on the rack in the corner. She felt cornered, and more than a little angry at Sam.

'You know, Sam,' she said sternly when she came back, 'I was hired as an editor, not a business adviser. As it's turned out, I've done just about every conceivable job around here for the past two years *except* any editing.'

'I know, I know,' he put in hastily. 'And I'm grateful. All that will change now. I promise you. Just do me this one last favour and from now on you can concentrate exclusively on editing. Period.'

She picked up the contract and gazed down at it with distaste. 'All right, I'll look it over, but I can't promise I'll understand it any more than you did. Can't you postpone this meeting with Stephen until John has had a chance to examine it?'

He shook his head vigorously. 'No. I can't. I don't know what there is about that guy. He was perfectly polite, didn't come on like the big boss or throw his weight around, but I had the distinct impression that when he said nine-thirty, he meant nine-thirty. You know what I mean?'

'Yes,' she murmured. 'I know what you mean.'

She brushed past him and went into her own cramped office, the desk still piled high with unread manuscripts. With a deep sigh, she sat down, put her elbows on top of the desk, her head in her hands, and started to plough her way through the hated document.

Half an hour later, she was so lost in the seemingly endless stream of convoluted legalese that she had no idea what she'd been reading, except for the one salient point, miraculously set out quite clearly: Stephen Kincaid was to have sole discretion over the expenditure of all monies contributed to the enterprise by his firm.

She raised her head and groaned aloud. And that was what Sam called a 'silent partner'! She could scarcely believe even he could be that dense. Of course, she knew what had happened. So long as Sam was confident Stephen wouldn't interfere with his editorial policies, he'd be satisfied and would sign anything.

She got up and stretched her cramped muscles. Was it really up to her to try to bail Sam out of the mess he'd got himself into? She was just about to march back into the reception room to tell him she was through, was resigning her job, when she heard the front door open and close, then the low hum of masculine voices.

Stephen! She'd forgotten. She glanced at her watch. Nine-thirty on the dot. There was no sense in delaying the inevitable. Best to get it over with as quickly as possible. She smoothed down the skirt of her suit, ran her fingers through her hair, picked up the contract, and went out into the reception room.

Both men stopped talking and turned to her at once when she came through the door. Sam's eyes were pleading, hopeful, Stephen's hooded and cold, his face giving away nothing.

'Good morning, Stephen,' she said brusquely.

He nodded briefly at her. 'Good morning.'

She flicked her eyes away from him quickly. He was dressed immaculately in a dark, beautifully tailored suit, crisp white shirt and deep red tie, and he looked wonderful, especially next to the rumpled Sam, who today hadn't even bothered to put on his one awful suit and tie.

'Well,' Sam said with false brightness, 'now that we're all here, shall we get started? Rachel, if you'll lock the door, I'll go and round up some chairs. Do you want coffee, Stephen? Doughnuts?'

Stephen shook his head. 'No, thanks.'

'Well, then, I'll be right back.'

When Sam was gone, Rachel walked over to the entrance door. Within the confines of the tiny room, she had to pass so close to Stephen that she could smell his familiar scent of tangy soap, mild after-shave. She turned the lock slowly, hoping Sam would come back before she had to face Stephen alone.

But she needn't have worried. He didn't utter another word until, a few minutes later, Sam came back carrying two battered chairs, one from her office, one from his. He set them near the one already there, towards which he beckoned Stephen.

After they'd seated themselves in a rough semi-circle, Rachel silently handed Sam the contract. It was his baby. Let him carry the ball. She was determined not to utter one word unless she had to. They both looked expectantly at Stephen, waiting. He had called the meeting, after all. It was up to him to start it rolling.

'The reason I wanted to meet,' he said smoothly, 'is to clarify a few details of our agreement.' He pointed at the contract, which Sam was clutching in his lap. 'I assume you've both had a chance to read it.'

Sam nodded. 'Oh, yes. It all seems—er—quite clear.'

Stephen's gray eyes flicked to her. 'Rachel?'

'Yes,' she said. 'I've read it, but I wouldn't say it's clear. I'm going to ask John to look it over.'

'It's a little late for that,' Stephen commented in a dry tone, 'since Sam has already signed it.'

'I think you and I both know,' she said evenly, 'that contracts can be broken if there's good cause.'

'Yes, you're right. But first one must prove good cause. Like fraud, misfeasance, bad faith.'

She nodded. 'Exactly.'

Of course they were both well aware that the contract they were really talking about was their own marriage vows. Although Rachel was remotely conscious of Sam's presence in the room, it was as though she and Stephen alone were conducting the conversation. In fact, glancing over at Sam now, and noticing the growing look of bewilderment on his face, she knew it was time to end the little personal by-play.

'In any event,' she said briskly, 'the one thing that seems set out in no uncertain terms is that the contract grants you, as your firm's representative, almost unlimited power over Sam's business.'

'That's true,' Stephen replied equably. 'And I think we have that right. It's our money we're risking, after all.' He turned to Sam. 'If you're worried about that aspect of it, Sam, you can put your mind at rest. I have no intention of interfering with your editorial policies. That's not my area of expertise.' He leaned back in his chair, crossed his long legs in front of him, and gave Sam the ghost of a smile. 'I have no quarrel with *what* you publish, but I think you'll have to admit your business practices have not been of the highest calibre.'

'You're right about that,' Sam said eagerly. 'In fact, I'll be glad of any help you can give me along those lines.'

Rachel had had enough by now of this male mutual admiration society, and she turned to Sam. 'I think you should wait, Sam, until John has had a chance to read the contract.'

'But, Rachel, why? I've already signed the thing. I can't see any problem.' He laughed and gave Stephen a conspiratorial wink. 'She's so suspicious. Doesn't trust anyone.'

Stephen gave her a long, hard look. 'I know,' he said curtly. Before she could say anything, he rose abruptly to his feet. 'Well, I think that just about covers it,' he said in a tone of finality. 'All I'll ask is that you let me examine your books once in a while and approve any expenditures, that kind of thing. I won't get in your way otherwise.' With another brief nod, he'd gone to the door, turned the lock, and stepped outside.

When he was gone, for some time there was utter silence in the small room. Finally, Sam turned to Rachel. 'Well?' he said with just a trace of defiance in his voice. 'It sounds all right to me.'

Slowly, she rose from her chair, then stood looking down at him. 'It's your baby, Sam,' she said. 'And your decision. In fact, now that the great mastermind has taken over, I'm going to forget all about business affairs and get going on that pile of manuscripts.'

She went back to her own office then, and stood by the side of the desk, staring into space for a long time. She felt let down by the brief meeting, and couldn't figure out why. Of course, Sam's craven toadying had been a disappointment, but it was more than that.

Then, suddenly, she knew. Aside from that one oblique reference to their divorce, their 'contract', he hadn't spoken one personal word to her, hadn't even given her a look that was just for her.

But that was what she wanted, wasn't it? Why be disappointed over that? What was wrong with her? Was she turning out to be one of those people who insisted on having their cake and eating it too? Why, oh why, had he had to come back?

Just then the telephone on her desk jangled, and she snatched it up. 'Hello.'

'Hi, Rachel, it's me,' came her sister's voice.

'Oh, hello, Laura.'

'Well?'

'Well what?'

'What happened last night?'

Rachel sank down in her chair. 'Nothing happened,' she replied. 'What did you expect?'

'Well, I saw the way he was looking at you all through dinner. There was no mistaking what was on *that* man's mind.'

Rachel sighed deeply. 'Laura, he spent the entire evening talking politics and sports with John.'

'Oh, I know all about that. That's not important. It's the *looks* he gave you I'm talking about.'

'Well, your extra-sensory powers failed you this time, sister, dear. As I said, nothing happened. But I do have a bone to pick with you.'

'Me?' Laura exclaimed innocently. 'What did I do?'

'You manoeuvred us both into what could have been a very embarrassing situation. Why didn't you tell me you'd invited Stephen for dinner? I wouldn't have come if I'd known, and you knew that.'

'Well, it was a last-minute thing,' Laura explained. 'He and John had lunch yesterday, and he drove John home, so John invited him in, and it just seemed the polite thing to do to ask him to dinner. I mean, after all, Rachel, he's my brother-in-law.'

'Not any more, he isn't,' Rachel said through her teeth. 'Now, will you please give it a rest? Don't you have enough to do with a nice husband like

John and four busy children, not to mention your adventures into cordon bleu cooking?'

'Yes, I guess I do,' Laura agreed shortly. 'And if that's what you really want——'

'It is.' It was obvious from Laura's tone of voice that she'd offended her. 'Believe me, Laura,' she added in a softer tone. 'It's really and truly all over between us.'

In the days and weeks that followed, Stephen, true to his word, kept his hands off Sam's business as far as any editorial decisions were concerned. In fact, he hardly showed up at the office at all—perhaps three times in one whole month—and then only to chat briefly with Sam or get his signature on a necessary document.

This of course freed Sam to do the work he was meant to do. Soon he'd lured back several of their old authors who had gone elsewhere, to other pub-lishers who actually *paid* them for their work. He was able to hire a receptionist-secretary and a bookkeeper, which in turn freed Rachel to concen-trate on her editorial duties.

The office was redecorated—not ostentatiously, but at least cleaned and painted. New furniture, smaller in scale, more streamlined, arrived for the reception room, which made it seem larger and definitely more impressive than its old dingy décor.

While all this was going on, Rachel kept pretty much to herself, stationed behind her desk in her newly painted office, making slow but steady prog-ress on the ever-growing stack of new manuscripts.

It was always a thrill to come across a promising new writer, and, for the first time in months, she actually began to enjoy her job.

Except for his rare visits to the office, during which she was able to avoid having to speak to him, Stephen made no further effort to contact her in any way. To all intents and purposes, he'd dropped out of her life completely.

It was May by now, usually one of Seattle's better months as far as weather was concerned, and one balmy evening after work Rachel decided it was about time she bought some new clothes. With the influx of money into the business, Sam was able to give her the rise she'd deserved for so long, and with spring in the air she found she had nothing suitable to wear.

After work one evening, then, she made her way to a small boutique she'd shopped at in the past. It carried the more conservative styles that she liked, and her favourite saleswoman still worked there, even remembered her.

She was looking through the lightweight suits for something in a spring-like colour when, at the end of the rack, she came face to face with Margaret Fulton, the last person on earth she ever wanted to see again.

Both women stopped short, and for a long moment simply stood there and stared at each other. She looked pretty much the same—just as lovely, her dark silky hair done up in a complicated twist on top of her head, the features still perfectly proportioned, the figure still slim.

'Hello, Margaret,' Rachel finally managed to blurt out.

'Hello, Rachel.' She paused a moment, then gave a tentative smile. 'It's been a long time.'

'Yes. How have you been?'

Margaret tossed her head. 'Oh, all right.' She laughed harshly. 'Married and divorced twice. That must be some kind of record for only two years.'

'Yes, well,' Rachel murmured politely. 'I guess I'll be on my way. Nice to have seen you.'

She turned to go, but before she could take a step she felt Margaret's hand on her arm, holding her back. Slowly she turned around to face her.

'Have a drink with me,' Margaret said. 'Please.'

Rachel didn't want to have a drink with her, didn't want to talk to her, was sorry she'd even run into her like this after two years of avoiding her. But there was something in Margaret's eyes that touched her, a pleading look. They'd been best friends all their lives up to two years ago, and all their common history wasn't that easy to forget, not completely.

'All right,' she said at last. 'One drink.'

CHAPTER FOUR

RACHEL and Margaret chose a popular restaurant lounge a few doors down the street. It was frequented mainly by working people from the nearby offices and shops, who would stop in for a quick drink after work before facing the gruelling commute to the suburbs.

It was past six o'clock by now, however. The commuter crowd had thinned considerably, and they were able to find a quiet table in the back right away.

Ordinarily not a drinker at all, when the waitress came to their table Rachel ordered a vodka martini. She didn't really like the taste, but, now that she was actually here, sitting across from Margaret Fulton, of all people, she was having serious second thoughts about the impulse that had prompted her to accept the invitation, and hoped a drink might help calm her jangling nerves.

They didn't have much to say while they waited for their drinks. Margaret seemed as nervous to Rachel as she was herself, her eyes darting around the room, picking a paper napkin to pieces, lighting a cigarette, then stubbing it out after a few puffs. All Rachel had on her mind by now was how soon she could decently take her leave.

When their drinks arrived, Margaret immediately raised her glass and took a long swallow of her Scotch and water. Then she lit another cigarette, put her elbow on the table, and leaned closer across it towards Rachel.

'I suppose you'd already heard that I was divorced recently.'

Rachel shook her head. 'No,' she murmured. 'I hadn't heard. I'm sorry.'

As the liquor did its work, Margaret seemed to relax visibly, while Rachel toyed with her glass, taking an occasional sip. She listened with only half an ear, still bent on getting out of there as soon as possible.

It wasn't long before Margaret finished her drink and held up a hand to a passing waitress to order another. She glanced at Rachel, who shook her head.

When her second Scotch arrived, Margaret took a healthy swallow, then gave Rachel a long look, her mouth twisted bitterly. 'Boy,' she said dully, 'I really know how to pick 'em. The first one was a drunken playboy, and the second one started fooling around the day we got back from our honeymoon.'

'I'm sorry,' Rachel said again. What else was there to say? You deserved it? You had it coming for what you did to me? Hardly; not at this late stage.

Margaret held up her glass in a mock toast. 'Well, here's to the single life!' she said in a brittle tone. 'It's the only way to fly.'

By now, she was slurring her words, and, as Rachel watched her, listening to the sad recital of her marital woes, she actually began to experience something like pity for her. In fact, it was only now that she noticed the hard lines in her face, the cynical glint to the still beautiful green eyes.

Of all the girls in their class in school, Margaret Fulton had been far and away the star. She was the prettiest, the smartest, the richest, the most popular, the best athlete. To see her come to this, drowning her disillusionment in Scotch, was a sad end to that early promise.

'Remember when we were girls?' Margaret was saying now. 'All those romantic notions we had about Mr Right! God, it seems like another lifetime ago.' She leaned closer and gave Rachel an intense, earnest look. 'But we did have some good times, though, didn't we?'

'Yes,' Rachel replied with a stiff smile. 'Of course we did.'

'Remember our first dance? How nervous we were, experimenting with make-up, wondering if anyone would ask us to dance? Remember how I stuffed newspaper in my bra to fill out my bosom in that low-cut dress? And how it crackled whenever I danced?'

Remember! Every sentence she uttered seemed to start with that word. And Rachel *did* remember—how Margaret had helped her fight off the bully who had tormented her in the schoolyard, how she had always seen to it that Rachel was chosen for the athletic activities she had no talent for, so she wouldn't be left out.

At the mention of the night they'd climbed out of Margaret's second-storey bedroom window and Rachel had got stuck in the branches of the willow tree, they were both helpless with laughter.

'And then, when Daddy called the fire department to unstick you and get you down on that ladder, how you sat there bawling and refused to budge.'

Rachel wiped away the tears of laughter as all the old memories came flooding back. It was all so long ago, yet it could have been only yesterday. When she raised her glass to take a sip of her drink, she was astounded to find it was empty! And that was her second one! It was definitely time to stop and go home.

She picked up her coat and bag and started to rise to her feet. 'Well,' she said, 'it's been nice seeing you again, Margaret, but it's really time I was getting home.'

'No,' Margaret said hastily, laying a hand on her arm. 'Not just yet. Please.'

Puzzled at the urgent tone in her voice, Rachel sank back down in her chair and waited while Margaret stared down into her drink—surely her fifth or sixth by now. Then she raised her head and turned towards Rachel without quite meeting her eyes.

'I hear Stephen's back in town,' she said casually.

Rachel stiffened. Immediately the mood was shattered and all the good will she'd begun to feel for her old friend vanished at the painful reminder.

'Yes,' she said shortly. 'He is.' She started to get up once again.

Margaret gave her a direct look this time, frowning. 'Oh, sit down, Rachel. It's taken me six drinks and two years to work up to this, and you're not leaving until I have my say.'

In spite of herself, Rachel was curious. 'All right,' she said, re-seating herself again. 'But make it quick, will you?'

'I'll try. You see, it's like this. That night...you know, the night of the party at your house when you came into the bedroom and saw us together. Well, I just want to tell you that it was entirely my idea. Stephen was only being polite.' She shrugged. 'I guess I was jealous. I mean, I'd always been the leader and you were the follower. It just didn't seem fair that you should walk off with a prize I couldn't have. I'm not proud of what I did, and I know I should have told you what really happened ages ago, at least before you actually divorced him. But it all happened so fast, and my precious pride was so deeply involved that I just couldn't make myself do it.'

Rachel listened intently to every word, and, as the full import of the sad tale slowly dawned on her, her one thought was that Stephen had been telling her the truth all along. It *hadn't* been his fault after all! Perhaps she should be angry at

Margaret for what she'd done, but instead she could have kissed her.

'Besides,' she was ending up miserably now, 'nothing actually happened. I mean, I'd stripped down somewhat and was pawing Stephen pretty strenuously, but he resisted—very politely—every step of the way.' She gave Rachel a hangdog look. 'So, that's how it was. Not only did I try to seduce your husband, but I managed to wreck your marriage in the process.' She took a deep breath. 'What I need to know is, can you ever forgive me?'

'Yes,' Rachel said quickly. 'Of course I forgive you.' She got up and stood for a moment looking down at her old friend. 'I'm grateful you told me. And I'm sorry for all your personal troubles. Now I really must go.'

She stumbled out of the restaurant into a pouring rain. Stopping only to shrug into her raincoat and tie a waterproof scarf over her head, she began walking, mindlessly, wherever the flow of other pedestrians took her.

All she could think of as she plodded along for what seemed like hours was what a fool she'd been. If only she'd stopped to listen to him two years ago! If only her pride, her insane jealousy hadn't stopped her from doing the rational thing at the time. Now it was too late.

But was it? She looked up to see that she was in front of the Four Seasons Hotel. Hadn't Stephen mentioned to John that night at dinner that he was staying there? It must be a sign! Her steps had taken her to the very place she unconsciously knew he would be.

She glanced at her watch. It was just past seven o'clock. Not as late as she'd thought. Chances were he'd be in. But what could she do? What was there to say? Well, the very least she could do was apologise to him. He'd said he still wanted her. Maybe it wasn't too late.

Quickly, before she could lose her nerve and change her mind, she marched through the revolving door into the lobby, then made her way over to the front desk. A clean-cut young man was behind it, and came over to her.

'Good evening,' he said with a smile. 'May I help you?'

'Yes, please. I'd like the number of Stephen Kincaid's room.'

'May I have your name?'

'Why?'

'I'll have to announce you.'

'But I don't want you to do that. I want to surprise him.'

'I'm sorry,' he said with an apologetic smile. 'It's hotel policy. You understand. For our guests' protection.'

'But in this case it won't be necessary,' she said hurriedly. 'I'm his wife.'

He raised an eyebrow and flipped open the registration book on top of the counter. 'I don't see any mention here of a Mrs Kincaid,' he said when he looked up again.

Rachel debated. The one thing she didn't want was for him to find out in advance that she was coming. It had to be a surprise or it wouldn't work at all. Then inspiration hit her.

Although she'd gone back to using her maiden name after the divorce, her driver's licence, good for eight years in Washington, was still in her married name. She fished her wallet out of her handbag, flipped it open to the licence, and shoved it across the desk at the clerk.

'Here,' she said, pointing. 'See? Rachel Kincaid.'

'Well . . .' he said dubiously.

'Please?' she said. 'Just the number of his room.'

'All right,' he said with a sigh. 'I shouldn't be doing this, but I guess if you really are his wife . . .'

At last he gave her the number of the room, which turned out to be a suite. She went over to the bank of lifts, got into an open car, and punched the button for the twenty-seventh floor. When she stepped out into the quiet corridor, it didn't take her long to find his door, since there were only four suites on that floor.

She hesitated before it for just a fraction of a second, then took a deep breath, raised her hand, and knocked. There was no reply. She knocked again, louder this time, praying he'd be there.

'Door's open,' she heard his voice call at last. 'Come on in.'

Slowly, fearfully, her heart pounding, her knees knocking, she turned the knob and pushed the door open. When she stepped inside the large sitting-room, she stood there for a moment, looking around. No one was there, but through a door she could hear the sound of running water. She couldn't think what to do, so she just stood there, waiting.

In just a few moments Stephen himself came sauntering into the room, and she drew in her breath, staring at him. He'd obviously just showered and shaved and was wearing only a pair of dark trousers, his chest and shoulders bare, and was wiping his face with a small hand towel.

When his eyes fell on her, he dropped his hands and stood stock-still, a frown creasing his face. Neither of them said a word for a long time. All she was aware of was the figure of the man himself, the broad bare chest, the wide, bony shoulders, the strong arms and flat stomach.

Finally he spoke. 'It's you,' he said.

She managed to force out a tremulous smile. 'Yes. It's me.'

'What do you want?'

Stalling for time, she walked slowly over to the window. She stood there for a moment gazing out at the lights of the city, the street far below glistening in the steadily pouring rain. So intensely aware was she of his silent presence behind her, obviously waiting for her to say something, that the back of her neck stared to tingle.

Finally, she turned around to face him. 'I just had a long talk with Margaret Fulton.'

He gave her a quizzical look, one dark eyebrow raised. 'Oh?' he said. 'And what did you two find to talk about?'

Finally her nerve snapped, and she stumbled across the room to stand before him, looking up at him, her eyes pleading. 'Oh, Stephen, can you ever forgive me? Margaret told me the truth about what happened that night, the truth you didn't want to tell me—that she was the one who forced herself on you, that you were only being polite to her. I've been such an idiot!'

'Yes,' he agreed quietly. 'You have.'

'Well, I'm grovelling, if that's what you want,' she said miserably. 'I'm begging your pardon.'

He nodded. 'All right. Apology accepted. Now, if that's all, I have a dinner date in just half an hour.'

She stared at him, struck dumb by the flat dismissal. But what else could she expect after the way she'd treated him? First accusing him of infidelity when he hadn't really done anything. Then divorcing him without even listening to what he had to say in his own defence, never once giving him the benefit of the doubt. Then, when he came back to her, wanting to try again, she'd rejected him.

'Yes,' she said quickly. 'Of course. I understand. Well, I just wanted to tell you...' She broke off with a shrug. 'You know.'

She turned then and, with a heavy heart, started towards the door. The ten feet or so she had to walk to get there seemed more like ten miles, and at the end of them was a perfect blank.

She had just put her hand on the knob, when she heard his voice. 'Rachel?' She turned around. He was walking towards her, slowly, his grey eyes glinting, a faintly amused smile playing about his thin mouth.

'Don't go,' he said quietly.

'But I thought you said——'

He waved a hand in the air. 'Never mind what I said. I didn't mean it.'

She stared at him for a moment, then the light dawned. 'You were punishing me,' she stated flatly.

'All right,' he admitted reluctantly. 'I guess I might have been. I guess I should apologise, but I think you owed me that.'

She had to laugh, in sheer relief if nothing else. 'You're right. I had it coming.'

'Well, then, come back and let's talk about it.'

All of a sudden, it was too much for her: the emotional conversation with Margaret, the martinis she'd drunk, working up the nerve to come here, his flat rejection. A wave of dizziness passed over her, she felt her knees buckle, and she closed her eyes, reaching out blindly for support.

The next thing she knew she was in his arms. He was holding her gently, patting her ineffectually on the back. She shook her head to clear it and looked up at him, forcing out a weak smile at the genuine look of concern in his eyes.

'Are you all right?' he murmured.

'Yes,' she said. 'At least, I think so.'

'Have you eaten anything?' he asked sternly.

She shook her head. 'No. There wasn't time.'

'A good thick steak is what you need, my girl,' he said sternly. 'I'll order us some dinner from Room Service.'

She eyed him carefully. 'I thought you had a dinner date.'

He shrugged. 'It's not important.'

He released her then and went over to the telephone, asked for Room Service, and proceeded to order two steaks, baked potatoes with all the trimmings, and a green salad. 'And lots of coffee,' he added.

'I think I'd better go and freshen up a little,' she said when he'd hung up.

'Good idea,' he replied. 'It's right down the hall.' The bathroom was still steamy from his shower, and the counter littered with his familiar toilet articles—shaving gear, toothbrush, the silver-backed hairbrush set she'd given him one Christmas. She wiped the mirror clear of steam and gazed at her reflection with a sinking feeling.

She looked like something the cat had dragged in and discarded, her hair still damp and flattened, every trace of wave long gone, her face bare of make-up, her eyes glazed. She washed her hands and splashed cold water on her face, then repaired the make-up as best she could with what she carried in her bag, and tried to tease her long tawny hair into some semblance of style.

Just as she was finishing up, she heard his low voice coming from the other room. She stood at the door, listening. He seemed to be talking on the telephone again, and, from the few words she could hear clearly, telling someone he wouldn't make it for dinner that evening after all.

She smoothed down her skirt, gave her hair one last comb through, then started back into the sitting-room. He'd put on a shirt while she'd been gone, and was just buttoning it up when she came into the room. His hands stilled, and they stood there for a few tense moments, simply staring at each other.

Just then there was a knock on the door, and a voice called out, 'Room Service, sir.'

Stephen opened the door, and a white-jacketed waiter wheeled in a trolley laden with their dinner. Stephen told him to place it on a small round table by the window, gave him a tip, and dismissed him.

When the waiter was gone, he turned to her. 'Well,' he said with a smile, 'shall we dine?'

'It smells wonderful,' she said, sniffing the air. 'But you did say you had other plans, and——'

'I told you it wasn't important,' he said shortly. 'Now let's get you fed before you faint on me again.'

'I did *not* faint,' she protested as she seated herself at the table. 'I never faint.'

He pulled up a chair to sit across from her. 'Oh, no? Funny, when you started to fall I somehow got that impression.' He lifted a fork and pointed it at her. 'You would have, too, if I hadn't caught you.'

'Well, maybe,' she admitted. 'I hadn't eaten since breakfast.'

He shook his head. 'You never did have much sense when it came to your feeding habits. Now, let's tuck in while it's still hot.'

Rachel started in on the delicious meal, reluctantly at first, only picking at her food, then with more gusto as the fluttery sensation in her stomach began to settle down. By the time she was halfway through her steak, her whole being had become suffused with a warm glow of happiness, a sensation that had been missing from her life for so long that she scarcely remembered what it felt like.

It wasn't only the fine meal, although food did help. It was far more the romantic setting, the luxurious suite, sitting by the window looking out at the city spread far below, and most of all it was being with Stephen again, knowing he cared, was concerned about her well-being, even her eating habits.

In this lovely glow, the dreadful two years they'd been apart simply melted away. This was where she belonged, and, in an odd way, the happiness she felt now was even better than before, because of that separation. It seemed to her now that she'd only been half alive then, that she was being raised as though from the dead, and that, if anything, her love for him was much deeper.

They didn't have much conversation during the meal. Rachel was content just to bask in the presence of the man she loved, had always loved, not to mention satisfying her hunger pangs, and Stephen seemed happy just to have her with him again.

After they'd finished, Stephen got up and crossed behind her to the small bar set in a small alcove off the main room.

'How about a glass of brandy?' he asked.

She twisted her head around to see him standing there, a bottle raised in one hand. 'No, thanks,' she said. 'I think I'll stick with coffee. It's wonderful.' She already felt half drunk on love. Liquor would only spoil it.

She turned back to pour another cup, smiling contentedly to herself as she listened to him pottering behind her at the bar, the clink of glass, the sound of the brandy bottle being replaced on the shelf.

Hearing the familiar sounds, knowing it was Stephen making them, brought tears to her eyes, tears of sheer joy. Blinking them away, she leaned back in her chair and gazed blindly out at the black night sky.

She sensed he had come up behind her even before she felt his touch. She'd known all along, of course, how the evening would end. In her eyes, he was still her husband, after all, and always had been. But now that it was here, her heart began to beat wildly in anticipation of what lay ahead.

At first, he only laid one hand lightly on her shoulder, as though waiting to see what her reaction would be before going further. Immediately she leaned her head down sideways so that her cheek rested on the back of his hand, and the grip tightened.

He reached in front of her to set his glass on the table, then put his other hand at the base of her neck, his fingers warm and soft on her skin. She held her breath, waiting. By now the very air seemed

to be crackling with the electricity their mutual
desire was generating between them.

The hand at her neck slipped lower, and when it
came to rest at the opening of her blouse, hovering
there, she felt as though her pounding heart would
leap out of her chest. His lips were on her cheek
now, his breath warm in her ear.

'God, how I've missed you!' he breathed.

'Oh, Stephen,' she cried, clutching at the hand
at her throat. 'I know.'

Unable to contain herself a moment longer, she
rose abruptly from her chair and turned around to
face him. Her eyes met his, glinting silvery now with
desire, and for several moments they stood there,
not touching, simply gazing hungrily at each other.

Then, with a low groan deep in his throat, he
reached out for her and she fell into his arms. It
felt so right to be held like this, every contour of
his long, hard body so familiar to her, and so dear,
that once again tears of happiness stung behind her
eyes.

He put a hand under her chin, tilting her face up
to hold her eyes with his, then, slowly, his open
mouth came down on hers. Her lips parted under
his, and as his tongue filled the inside of her mouth
the taste of him, the feel of him set every nerve in
her body tingling, filling her with naked desire.

When the hand under her chin moved downwards, to the base of her throat, past the opening
of her blouse, to settle on her breast, she closed
her eyes and breathed a deep sigh of pure con-

tentment. He tore his mouth away and looked down at her again.

'I want you, Rachel. More than ever. Say you want me, too.'

'Oh, darling,' she cried, throwing her arms around his neck. 'Of course I want you.'

He drew back from her then and his fingers started fumbling with the buttons of her blouse. She stood quite still, allowing him the pleasure of undressing her, a significant aspect of their old lovemaking. Soon the blouse was pulled down over her shoulders to reveal the slip underneath.

'Ah,' he said, slipping one strap over her shoulder. 'Still don't wear a bra, I see.'

She reddened, self-consciously muttering something about her rather meagre endowments in that quarter. He sensed her discomfiture immediately, and placed a hand on her breast as though to reassure her. 'I love your endowments,' he said, moving his hand sensuously from one small firm mound to the other. 'I always have.'

As though to prove his point, he then pulled both straps down and bent his head to kiss her breasts, his mouth lingering over each thrusting peak, his tongue and lips playing lightly with them. She clutched at the dark head and threw her head back, giving herself up totally to the moment, her growing desire for him almost painful.

After a moment he left her to shrug out of his own shirt, then pressed her to him once again, their bare flesh meeting. His hands clutched at her hips, pulling her tighter, and she could feel his hard arousal against her thigh, a sure sign of her power over him.

He unzipped the back opening of her skirt and slowly pulled it down over her hips, her legs, his hands and mouth lingering over each inch of revealed flesh. Then he picked her up in his arms and as he carried her she raised her hands up around his neck, placing her lips against the bare skin of his broad chest, the muscles quivering under her mouth.

At the door to the bedroom he stopped, and she raised her head to look up at him questioningly. 'Are you sure, Rachel?' he asked in a low voice. 'Is this what you want?'

'Oh, Stephen, can you doubt it?' she replied. She smiled. 'You said it yourself. This was one department where we never did have a problem.'

'No,' he said, moving forward again.

He laid her down on top of the bed, and began to strip off the rest of his clothes. She gazed hungrily at him from the shadows as his body was gradually revealed in the flickering glow of the red and blue neon lights from the building across the street.

When he was naked, he lay down beside her and took her in his arms. Her heart was so full of love for him that she wanted somehow to find a way to make it up to him for the two years she'd kept them apart, and now, lying in his arms, she knew what it was.

She raised herself up on one elbow and leaned over him. 'Stephen,' she said breathlessly.

'What is it?' He reached out a hand and moved it across her bare breasts, then lower, over her stomach, her thighs.

'Let me make love to you.'

For a moment he seemed somewhat taken aback. Then he smiled, withdrew his hand, and slowly sank back on the pillow, his arms crossed behind his head. 'My pleasure,' he said simply.

But she didn't get far. She had meant to seduce him slowly, using her hands and mouth to arouse him, but she soon found it wasn't going to work. By the time she'd reached the line of coarse hair that started on his lower abdomen, he had groaned pitifully and reached out for her, raising her up so that she hovered above him, her hair falling around her face.

'Stop it,' he growled. 'I can't take any more.'

Swiftly, he twisted around so that he was now above her. She closed her eyes and sank into pure sensation as his own lips and hands did their work on her, until finally she too could stand no more, and, clutching at him, her fingernails digging into his back, she cried aloud.

'Oh, now, darling. Please, now.'

He raised his head and gazed down at her, then slowly covered her body with his, and they were joined together again, husband and wife.

Some time during the night, Rachel woke up with a start to the loud piercing sound of a wailing siren. She sat bolt upright, listening as it passed by then faded into the distance, her mind in a daze, clutching the covers around her naked shoulders.

Then she remembered. She looked over at the familiar dark head on the pillow next to her. He still slept in the same old posture, on his stomach, his arms raised and resting beside his head. The covers were tangled around his waist, and the flickering red and blue lights across the street intermittently revealed his strong back and shoulders.

She ached to reach out to him, to smooth the tousled black hair, straighten the covers, run her hand down that smooth bare back. But she didn't want to disturb him. For several long moments she simply gazed down at him, her heart overflowing with love.

This was Stephen, she kept reminding herself. Her husband, who was lost and now returned to her. With a happy sigh, she slipped carefully out of bed so as not to waken him, then padded, naked and barefoot, out of the bedroom and across the hall to the bathroom.

She turned on the shower, and while she waited for the water to heat she glanced at herself in the mirror. Her eyes were glazed, her mouth swollen, and her hair in a fine mess. She picked up his comb from the counter and ran it through the tangles; then, with the one pin remaining in it, tucked it up on top of her head.

She stepped inside the shower stall and stood under the warm spray for a long time, her face lifted up to it, her eyes closed, lost in happy recollections of their lovemaking, every wonderful detail. And there was the future to think about, too. They'd have to discuss that later.

Just then she was startled out of her reverie by the sound of the bathroom door opening and closing. Then the glass door to the shower opened as well, and Stephen appeared on the other side, his eyes still a little sleepy.

'I was wondering where you'd gone,' he said.

'Oh, not far. Don't worry. You won't lose me that easily.'

'When I heard the shower, I thought you might need some help,' he said with a wicked grin.

'Oh, I can always use assistance,' she replied in a mock serious tone.

He stepped inside to stand behind her in the narrow space and reached for the soap. In a moment his lathery hands, slippery with soap, came around to stroke up and down her body as she leaned back against him. It wasn't long before the tension began to build between them yet again, and his hands stilled on her breasts.

'Had enough?' he murmured in her ear.

In reply, she turned around and threw her arms around his neck, drawing his head down, clutching the damp hair at the back of his neck. As their lips met, together they sank slowly down on the tiled floor.

CHAPTER FIVE

THE next morning they had a late, leisurely breakfast in the suite, sitting across from each other at the same table by the window, enjoying a pale sunshine. Thankfully, it was Saturday, so there wouldn't be any need to explain her absence from work to Sam.

'What would you like to do this weekend?' he asked between healthy bites of bacon and eggs.

'Oh, I don't know,' she replied. She wouldn't mind just staying in the hotel, so long as they were together.

'Since it looks like a pretty decent day weather-wise,' he went on, 'I was thinking we might drive up over Snoqualmie Pass, see the last of the winter snow or the spring wild flowers in bloom or something. The company keeps a suite in the lodge. We could stay there.'

'Sounds fine. I'll have to go home first to change.'

He nodded. 'No problem.' He got up and came over to her, putting a hand on her shoulder. 'Think I'll go and shower while you finish up your breakfast.'

She looked up and gave him an intimate smile. 'But you already showered last night. Remember?'

'Oh, yes,' he said in a low voice. He slid his hand down and slipped it inside her blouse. 'But, if you'll recall, there was quite a bit of energetic activity afterwards.'

His touch on her breast sent shivers up and down her spine. 'Yes,' she said breathlessly. 'I remember quite well. And unless you intend to indulge in that activity again, I suggest you get yourself under that shower right away. Perhaps a cold one would be in order.'

Reluctantly he withdrew his hand. 'You're right. It's just that it's been so long. We have a lot of lost time to make up for.' He bent down and gave her a quick kiss on the cheek, then walked off, whistling soundlessly under his breath.

While he showered, Rachel picked away at her breakfast. She wasn't really hungry, but supposed she should eat something. She kept reliving the previous night, the happiest night of her life. He'd never been so tender, so loving, so anxious to fulfil her needs as well as his own. If their lovemaking had been satisfying when they were married, it was sheer heaven now.

Yet something nagged at the back of her mind, a little worm of concern eating away where she couldn't quite get at it. But what could possibly spoil their happiness now? She'd learned the truth about what she'd thought was his old infidelity with Margaret, she'd admitted her mistake, he'd forgiven her. They were both free to take up their lives where they'd left off two years ago. What could possibly go wrong?

Then it hit her. Not once, not even at the very height of passion, had he said he loved her. She knew he did; there was no question about it in her mind. Then why didn't he say so? Nor had he mentioned anything about their future.

Just then she heard his voice coming from the bathroom, over the noise of the shower. He was singing! A little off-key, to be sure, and not getting in all the right words to the popular tune he'd chosen, but he'd always sung in the shower when he was happy.

She gave herself a little shake. How silly of her to start brooding like that! And all over nothing! If he hadn't actually said he loved her or offered any suggestions about their future plans, he would in time. It was too soon. After all, he'd been hurt too. In time they'd work out all the necessary practical details. And the one thing that was an absolute certainty in her mind was that they would be together.

After stopping at her house to change her clothes and pick up a few things, they headed towards the mountains. It was a glorious day, with the winter's snows still sparkling on the higher reaches of the towering, tree-covered Cascade Range. There were even a few late skiers at the very summit.

The lodge was a new one she'd never been to before, and the company's suite sinfully luxurious. They took long walks, lingered over delicious meals, sat in front of the fire that night with the remaining ski bunnies, and then spent a long night of love-making in their room overlooking the mountain slope, the snow brilliant under a full moon.

They started back to the city late on Sunday afternoon, and as he drove she laid her head on his shoulder, one hand resting on his knee. She loved the feel of the powerful thigh muscles under the rough material of his jeans. He was so vital, so alive. And he'd brought her to life again. She was nothing without him. She knew that now.

But even in this mood of near-perfect contentment, now that they were on their way back to civilisation and the humdrum round of everyday affairs the little doubts she'd felt yesterday morning began to nag at her again.

He still hadn't told her he loved her, nor mentioned any aspect of their future beyond the next activity, whether it was a meal, a walk, or making love. He was simply existing in the present—a faculty he'd always had, and one that she couldn't share. She had to have some idea what was ahead. Most likely he was leaving it up to her, since she was the one who'd left him, after all. But how to broach the subject?

It wasn't until they were back in the city that she finally saw her chance. While he waited for the light to change at the first main intersection after leaving the inter-state, he turned to her.

'Where to? Do you want to go home, or shall we go back to the hotel? We could have dinner. First, that is,' he added, with a wicked smile. He reached over to put a hand on her knee, and the grey eyes gleamed at her. 'Of course, you know what I prefer.'

The light changed just then, and as he pulled ahead into the traffic Rachel's mind raced. She didn't know how to answer him. They did have to talk, and driving in a car wasn't the place to do it.

'I have an idea,' she said at last. 'If you'll stop at a grocery store I can pick up some steaks and cook dinner at home. How does that sound?'

'Sounds great,' he replied promptly, and made the turn that led to her house.

They were just finishing dinner when she finally decided to take the plunge.

They were sitting at the table in the kitchen, which overlooked the back garden, in full bloom now with rhododendrons, azaleas and the tulip bulbs she had planted last autumn. It all seemed so familiar to her, and so right to have him sitting across from her again in their own home.

'Ah, that was great,' he said when he'd swallowed the last bite. 'I'm happy to see you're still such a wonderful cook.'

'I'm glad you enjoyed it. How about some coffee?'

'Yes, I'd like some.'

She got up and went to the counter, and while she measured out the coffee and ran the water she searched her mind for a good way to broach the subject while she still had the nerve. But why should she be nervous? They loved each other. They belonged together.

When the coffee began to drip, she turned around to face him. 'I've been thinking,' she said slowly.

'There's not much point in your going back to the hotel. In fact,' she went on, 'you might as well check out and move in with me now.'

He gave her a startled look, then laid his fork carefully down on his plate. He leaned back in his chair, gazing out of the window, apparently deep in thought.

As Rachel watched him, waiting for him to say something, a little knot of fear began to form in the pit of her stomach. Something was obviously troubling him. What could it be? Had she said the wrong thing, made a *faux pas* of some kind?

Finally, he turned back to her. 'I don't know if that would be such a good idea,' he said carefully.

She gave him a tremulous smile and tried to put a playful note into her voice. 'Don't tell me you've developed Victorian scruples. Are you going to insist on making an honest woman of me before we start living together publicly again?'

He frowned. 'I can see we've got a few things to talk over,' he said.

He pushed his chair back, got up from the table, and went over to stand in front of the window, his hands shoved in the back pockets of his trousers. As she watched him, Rachel's apprehension began to escalate into alarming proportions. She felt she should do something, say something—go to him, perhaps—but a warning voice in her head told her to sit still and wait.

Eventually he turned around and came back to the table. Slowly, he poured himself a fresh cup of coffee, took a long swallow, then set the cup down, taking his chair again and giving her a long, close look.

'I think we might have been operating a little at cross purposes here,' he began. 'It sounds as though you have the idea that we'll remarry.'

'Well, yes,' she said in a halting voice. 'I guess that's true. What else, after what's happened between us? I mean, yes, I just assumed ... that is, I thought ...'

He shook his head slowly from side to side. 'I'm sorry, Rachel,' he said. 'I thought I made it crystal-clear to you weeks ago—in fact, that first day at lunch—that another marriage to anyone was definitely not part of my future, that I just didn't believe in second chances.'

'Well, yes,' she said. 'But you were talking about *second* marriages.'

He smiled thinly. 'Well, what would you call it if we were to marry again?'

'But that doesn't count if it's with the same person!'

He threw back his head and laughed harshly. 'I see your arithmetic is still as shaky as ever. Whether it's to two different people or the same person, it still counts as a second marriage.'

'But ...' She stopped short, aware suddenly of the whining note in her voice. She was begging, and it was useless. There was no budging him once his mind was made up.

She simply stared at him, open-mouthed. 'But what about last night?' she stuttered at last. 'And the night before that? Didn't that mean anything?'

'Of course it did,' he said hastily, reaching across the table to put his hand over hers. 'It was wonderful. Just the way it used to be. Even better. And I'm sorry if I misled you about my intentions.'

'But I don't understand,' she said. 'I thought after my talk with Margaret straightened out my own misconception about the past there wouldn't be a problem. As soon as I realised I'd been in the wrong, the first thing I did was come to you. I admitted my mistake, I apologised humbly, I begged your forgiveness. And I thought you'd granted it.'

'I did,' he assured her hurriedly. 'You know I did.'

'What you're saying, then, is that you don't love me,' she intoned flatly.

'Not at all. I *do* love you, in my way. I just don't believe in marriage any more. Remember, Rachel, I was hurt too. Oh, yes,' he added grimly, 'I can be hurt.'

She was growing angry by now. He'd placed her in such an awkward, humiliating position! It was almost as though he'd betrayed her trust all over again. She jumped to her feet and stood glaring down at him.

'After all, Stephen,' she said in a tight voice, 'you were the one who came back to Seattle, sought me out, wangled your way into Sam's business for just that purpose, I might add.'

'Rachel,' he said wearily, 'sit down. Please sit down. We need to talk this out sensibly, like two mature adults. Don't fly off the handle until you hear what I have to say.'

Slowly she sank back down in her chair. The one thing she didn't want to do was burst into tears or go stalking out in a huff. He was right about one thing. It was absolutely imperative that they talk it out and see where they stood. She'd never forgive herself if she made the same mistake twice.

'All right,' she said. 'I'm listening.'

'You seem to think that the issue of Margaret was the sole cause of our problems, that once that was resolved to your satisfaction we could simply take up where we'd left off.'

'Well,' she bit out, 'didn't we? I don't know what else you'd call what's been going on between us lately.'

He flushed deeply. 'All right. Maybe I was wrong. Maybe I took too much for granted. I guess I just assumed that you had no more interest in a permanent commitment than I did, especially now that your job with Sam offers a more promising future for your career.'

'I don't know how you can say that,' she said in an insistent voice. 'I loved our marriage! And as far as I was concerned, everything was perfect until I thought you spoiled it by going to bed with my best friend. Now that I realise that didn't happen, I simply don't see the problem.'

He gave her a long, penetrating look. 'Don't you? Was our marriage really so fine? Think back a minute, Rachel, to the time before that one isolated episode.'

Watching him, Rachel began to recognise the familiar tell-tale signs of his own growing anger:

the set jaw, the pulse throbbing along his jawline, the fists clenched on top of the table. She opened her mouth to argue the point, but he obviously hadn't finished. He raised a hand to stop her, and leaned forward, the grey eyes glinting narrowly at her.

'Try asking yourself a few probing questions about your own behaviour, long before Margaret came along.'

'Like what?' she said in a tight voice.

'Like, who was so jealous of my success that she insisted on striking out on a half-baked career of her own instead of staying home and being a wife? Who refused to have children until she'd proved herself in that wonderful career?' He shook his head. 'It wasn't working long before Margaret came along, and, if you'll be honest with yourself for once in your life, you'll admit it.'

Rachel's head was whirling by now. All she wanted now was to get him out of there as quickly as possible, to banish those accusing eyes, the hurtful accusations, the flat rejection. And he was dead wrong, anyway. None of the things he was saying was true. He was only trying to defend his own bad behaviour. Just like a man, she thought furiously. The best defence is a good offence.

Well, she wasn't having any. Her life had been going quite well before he came back into it, and it would do so again. Mustering up all her dignity, she rose slowly from her chair, gave him a pitying look.

'All right, Stephen,' she said in a steady voice that was edged with steel. 'If that's the way it seems to you, then I don't think we have anything more to say to each other. Now, I think you'd better leave.'

Slowly he rose to his feet and gave her a long, penetrating look, raising a hand towards her, then letting it drop to his side. 'I don't want to lose you, Rachel,' he said in a low voice.

She gave him a withering glance. 'Well, that's too bad, Stephen, because you just did.'

She turned from him then, and went over to the window. She stood there rigid and unmoving, every muscle in her body tense, her hands clenched into fists at her sides.

There was total silence in the room for a long time, then, when she heard him start to leave, it took all her will-power not to turn around and go to him. But she didn't do it. He'd humiliated her for the last time.

He hadn't been gone fifteen minutes when the telephone began to shrill loudly in the silent house. She was still standing where he'd left her, gazing blankly out into the garden, which was filled with shadows now that the sun was setting.

At first she decided not to answer it. There was no one she wanted to talk to. It couldn't possibly be Stephen. Or could it? Just on the off chance, she ran into the living-room and snatched up the receiver.

'Hello.'

'Where have you been?' came her sister's indignant voice. 'I've been worried sick about you.'

Rachel slumped down in the chair beside the table, groaning inwardly. 'Oh, for heaven's sake, Laura,' she said. 'I just went away for the weekend.'

'Where? Who with?'

'Laura, back off,' she replied in a warning tone. 'I'm not ten years old. I don't need you to monitor my every movement. Can't you give me a little credit for handling my own life the way I think best?'

There was total silence on the line then. Rachel knew she'd offended her sister, and, although she guessed she should be sorry about that, at this point she didn't much care.

'Well, all right,' Laura said huffily at last. 'I'm sorry.' She paused, but only long enough to latch on to a new idea. 'You went away with Stephen, didn't you?'

'What makes you think that?'

'Well, I know you quite well, Rachel. At least well enough to realise there's not another man on earth you *would* go off with.'

Rachel heaved a sigh. Considering the highly efficient grape-vine Laura was in tune with, she was going to find out anyway. 'All right,' she said at last. 'You win. I "went off" with Stephen, as you so delicately put it.'

'Well, good for you!' Laura replied with feeling. 'So what's the plan?' she went on eagerly. 'Will you remarry right away—or what?'

Rachel gritted her teeth. 'There is no plan, and there's not going to be any marriage.'

'Why on earth not? You love him, don't you? And he still loves you. What's the problem?'

She might as well come out with it now and get it over with. Laura wouldn't give her a moment's peace until she found out, and Rachel knew quite well that she'd manage to worm it out of her eventually.

'The problem is, sister dear, that he doesn't want to.'

'I don't believe that for a minute!' was the immediate reply. 'What makes you think that?'

Rachel gave a harsh laugh. 'Because he said so, that's what. In no uncertain terms, I might add.'

'Well, what *does* he want, then?' Laura demanded in a tone of exasperation.

'Who knows? An affair, I suppose.'

'Oh, drat men, anyway! Aren't they the limit?'

Rachel had to smile. With a loyal, faithful, devoted husband like John, Laura had no experience whatsoever of the foibles of a more feckless breed of men.

But her sister hadn't finished and was still talking. 'I just don't understand——'

'Listen, Laura,' Rachel broke in. 'I know you mean well, but I really don't feel much like discussing it at the moment. I'm dead tired. I'll call you tomorrow. OK?'

'Yes, of course,' Laura assured her in a subdued tone. 'But I just want to say one more thing. Is that all right?'

'Go ahead. What is it?'

'Just that if you really want him, you may have to fight for him. Now, goodnight. And don't fret. It'll all work out.'

Oh, sure it will, Rachel thought as she hung up. Laura might have her romantic illusions, but such dreams were over for her.

For the next few weeks, although Rachel awoke every morning with a still painfully deep sense of loss, she was so busy at her job that she didn't have time to brood over her now non-existent personal life. Even Laura, bless her heart, had kept her promise and never raised the subject again.

As word got around that Overton Publishing was now a going concern again, paying top rates for material, her work, by necessity, became the main focus of her life. She spent long hours poring over the really excellent manuscripts submitted to them now, in the office as well as in the evenings at home, and consulting with their growing list of fine writers.

In fact, it was her work that saved her sanity over the next few difficult weeks. Whenever her thoughts began wandering back towards Stephen and the weekend they'd spent together, she'd simply focus them back on the manuscript she was reading, the writer she needed to consult with, the contract to be drawn up.

Sam was just as overworked as she was, but he too seemed to thrive on it. Since his area of expertise was layout work, dealing with artists and printers, he was gone from the office more than he was there, and their paths didn't cross often.

Although the ache in her heart never quite left her, at last the morning finally came when she woke up with the realisation that the worst of her misery had pretty well dissipated. By now it was almost three weeks since she'd last seen Stephen, and she hadn't heard a word from him or about him. Clearly he had no intention of trying to contact her again. She'd made her feelings quite plain, and so had he, and that was the end of it.

The day dawned bright and clear, the morning sun streaming through her bedroom window, the birds singing in the tall Douglas fir tree at the corner of the house, and when she opened the window she could smell the powerful scent of the lilac just coming into bloom.

After all, she mused as she showered and dressed for work, she'd forgotten him once, and she could do it again. The worst of it had been the humiliation. Even now the memory of how she had given herself to him so unreservedly throughout that weekend could fill her with shame. He'd used her, then rejected her.

Well, maybe she had had it coming. It was her own stupid pride and blind jealousy that had wrecked the marriage in the first place. You could hardly blame him for not wanting to risk that again. And she had to admit that some of the things he'd accused her of that day were probably true.

She *had* been jealous of his success, wanted to try her wings at a career of her own, even put off

having children when he wanted them, because of
it. What she couldn't forgive him now, however,
was that he had seduced her into believing he still
loved her, just to get her into bed.

But there was no point brooding over what
couldn't be helped. It was over—for good this time.
And perhaps the pain of loneliness was preferable
to the pain love seemed to bring her.

Sam was in the office when she stepped inside the
small, newly painted reception room. That was a
surprise, but she received an even bigger shock when
he turned around to greet her.

'Sam?' she said, goggling at him. 'Is it really
you?'

Not only was his flaming, unruly red hair cut in
an obviously expensive layered style, but he was
wearing a well-tailored dark grey suit, a quietly
striped blue and white shirt, and a deep-rust-
coloured tie that just matched his hair.

He gave her a shamefaced smile and shrugged
his shoulders. 'Well, now that I'm going to be a
big-shot executive, I thought I'd better start dressing
the part.'

'But you look wonderful!' she cried, walking up
to him. 'Why, you've even had a manicure.'

He shoved his hands quickly into his trouser
pockets, his face brick-red by now. 'Oh, come on,
Rachel,' he said with a frown. 'Lay off.'

She laughed. 'I don't know why you should be
so embarrassed. You look gorgeous. I never
dreamed such a handsome, elegant man lurked be-

neath the old rough exterior. I'm really impressed, Sam.'

He grinned at her. 'Do you really mean it?'

She nodded her head vigorously. 'Absolutely.'

'Well, you know, I do need to make an impression now that we're going to be playing in the big leagues.'

'I agree. In fact, I was thinking I could use a new wardrobe myself, and now that you're paying me what I'm worth I might go on a shopping spree of my own.'

The fleeting thought crossed her mind that she'd been doing just that when she'd run into Margaret Fulton, and at the memory of what had happened afterwards she could feel herself reddening again. Before Sam could notice anything wrong, she reached up to straighten his tie which, even in his new sartorial splendour, was still a little crooked.

'There,' she said, giving the knot a final pat. 'Now you're perfect.'

As he looked down at her his grin gradually faded, and his expression took on a more sober cast. 'Perfect enough to be seen out to dinner with me?'

His tone was light, but Rachel knew he was dead serious, and she was taken somewhat by surprise. She'd always turned him down when he'd asked her out in the past; not because of his appearance, but because she'd resisted getting involved with any man during those two years she and Stephen were separated.

In fact, she had to wonder now if the underlying truth about that resistance wasn't that she had still

harboured the secret hope of an eventual reconcili-
ation with Stephen. Now that dream was shattered
for good. Perhaps it was time she spread her wings.
While she couldn't conceivably envisage a romance
with Sam, she liked him a lot and felt very
comfortable with him.

'Sam,' she said hesitantly, 'I've been totally open
and honest with you about my feelings——'

He held up a hand, cutting her short. 'I know,
I know,' he said with a rueful shrug. 'I just thought
I'd try again.' He grinned. 'I figured now that I'm
more presentable you might change your mind. But
I understand.'

'But Sam, I'm not saying I won't have dinner
with you,' she said with a smile.

His eyebrows shot up. 'You're not?'

'No. I just want to make it clear beforehand that
I'm not in the market for any kind of—well, in-
volvement, attachment, whatever you want to call
it . . . especially with someone I work with.'

'Fine!' he exclaimed fervently. 'I can relate to
that. I'm a pretty confirmed bachelor myself, you
know. But since we're both footloose and fancy-
free, there's no reason why we shouldn't have some
fun together. Right?'

'No reason at all,' she agreed with a straight face.

'So, you'll go out to dinner with me?'

She nodded. 'Yes.'

'When?'

She laughed. 'Well, you're doing the asking. Why
don't you pick the time?'

'All right,' he replied promptly. 'Today's Monday. How about Wednesday?'

She hesitated. Wasn't that too soon? Then she thought, why not? She had to get started some time. 'All right,' she agreed. 'Wednesday. Why don't you pick me up at my place around seven?'

'Agreed.'

'Now we'd both better get to work if we're going to earn the money our new masters are paying us.'

All that morning she kept wondering if she'd made a mistake in agreeing to the dinner date with Sam. He seemed to understand her firm determination to avoid any emotional entanglements, but she knew quite well that very often what a person said and what he meant were two different things. She'd done all she could to make her position clear, however, and if he chose to put his own interpretation on it she couldn't be held responsible.

They'd have this one quiet dinner together, at any rate, just to celebrate Sam's new image, and then she'd see.

Rachel was quite surprised at the place Sam chose to have dinner on Wednesday night. She'd simply assumed that with his new elegant image he'd try to impress her by taking her to one of the more exclusive—and expensive—restaurants in town. Instead, they ended up at a noisy, smoky, rather rowdy tavern in the university district.

'This place is one of my old college hang-outs,' he shouted in her ear as they made their way through the crowd. 'Hope you don't mind, but I feel at home here.'

'No, I don't mind,' she shouted back at him over her shoulder. 'It looks like fun.'

Country music was blaring loudly from the juke-box, some cowboy wailing nasally about his lost love. The long wooden bar was crowded with people, mostly men drinking foaming mugs of beer. There was the pungent aroma of pizza in the close air, warm from the press of bodies on all sides.

It was a little quieter in the back room, where the dining tables were set up. As soon as they sat down, a young waiter in a rather grimy white apron and balancing a tray in one hand came briskly up to the table.

'What'll it be, Sam?' he asked briskly. 'The usual?'

'You got it, Jerry,' Sam replied. 'Only make it a double portion.' He winked and flicked a glance across the table at Rachel. 'Got a hot date tonight.'

'Sam,' she said, when Jerry had trotted off, 'I don't know what you meant by that last remark, but——'

'Oh, come on, Rachel. Lighten up. I was only kidding.'

She gave him a suspicious look, but, when she saw the broad grin spread all over his face, the glow of happiness in the light blue eyes, she realised he'd only been showing off. In fact, it was actually rather flattering to be considered a 'hot date' after all these years of solitary meals.

'All right, but just don't get any ideas.'

He threw up his hands and gave her a look of total innocence. 'Absolutely not!' he exclaimed fervently.

As it turned out, Rachel ended up having a wonderful time. Sam was a very relaxing person to be around, and the surroundings were so informal, so friendly that by the end of the evening she was joining in the community singing with real relish.

When they left it was past eleven o'clock, and as they ambled leisurely towards Sam's car they were still laughing at the events of the evening.

Inside the car, Sam turned to her. 'Now,' he said firmly, 'for being such a good sport and entering into *my* world, I'm going to reward you by taking you for a last drink in yours.'

'What do you mean?' she asked, settling herself comfortably.

He started the car and pulled out into the street. 'We're going to the Space Needle.'

'Oh, Sam,' she protested. 'Don't you think it's a little late for that? We both have to work tomorrow, you know.'

'Yes,' he said, waggling his ears at her. 'But I'm the boss, remember?'

'All right,' she said with a laugh. 'If it'll make you happy. But I enjoyed your world, as you call it, very much.'

It wasn't the usual thing to ride up the glass-enclosed lift to the top of the revolving Space Needle just for one drink, but somehow Sam managed to bluster his way past the disapproving eyes of the *maître d'hôtel* to the bar.

They stood at the entrance of the dimly lit room, searching for a table, but they all seemed to be taken, and there was no room at the bar. Just then, way in the back, two men got up, threw some money down on the table, and began to walk slowly towards them, still deep in conversation.

'Ah, a table,' Sam crowed in her ear. 'Let's grab it before that snooty *maître d'* gives it to someone else.'

He placed both hands on her shoulders, propelling her forward so that she almost bumped into a passing waiter. Frowning, she turned around to protest.

'Don't push me like that, Sam. I nearly collided with that waiter.'

'Better you than me,' he said, waggling his ears again, and she had to laugh.

Still smiling, she turned around and began to move forward again, but, before she got far, one of the two men who were just leaving moved aside to allow her to pass by in the narrow aisle. Rachel glanced over to thank him, and in the sudden blaze of light from the dining-room she found herself looking directly into the startled grey eyes of Stephen Kincaid.

CHAPTER SIX

FOR a moment the three of them simply stood there, blocking the passageway, staring at each other. It was Stephen who collected himself first.

'Rachel,' he said, with an abrupt nod. 'Sam.' He paused. 'You two look as though you're having a big night out on the town.'

'That's right,' Rachel said quickly.

'Not really,' Sam said at exactly the same time.

Rachel could have murdered him on the spot. It wouldn't hurt Stephen to believe it was a real date, even a romantic evening. She did notice, however, the frank appraisal Stephen was making of Sam in his new finery, and that gave her some satisfaction.

Stephen's mouth curled in amusement. 'You don't seem to be too sure which it is,' he commented in a mocking tone.

Sam, looking utterly bewildered by the whole episode, flicked a glance at Rachel, then at Stephen, until finally a light seemed to dawn. 'Er—yes,' he finally managed to stutter out. 'I guess you could say that. I mean, that Rachel and I are having a night out on the town.'

Stephen turned to his companion. 'You go on ahead, Larry. I'll join you in a moment.' Then he looked at Sam, ignoring Rachel completely. 'Actually, I'm glad I ran into you. I have to go to New

York first thing tomorrow morning and will be gone for several days. If you need to get hold of me, you have my office number there.'

'Yes. Sure,' Sam said.

Stephen nodded again then, and walked off. When he was gone, Sam gave Rachel a long, hard look. She tried to avoid his eyes, but knew it was hopeless.

'So,' he said at last. 'What was that all about?'

'What?'

'Oh, come on, Rachel, I'm not blind, you know. I thought you told me there was nothing between you any more.'

'There isn't,' she replied promptly.

Sam shook his head slowly from side to side. 'Well, it sure didn't look that way to me.' Then suddenly he glanced past her and frowned. 'Damn,' he muttered. 'Someone's got our table.'

'Oh, Sam,' she said. 'I don't really think I want a drink after all. Why don't we just go home now?'

'Look,' he said, 'there are two vacant seats at the bar. Let's just have one drink now that we're here.'

Actually, she didn't want to leave quite yet anyway, for fear of running into Stephen again. By the time they had one drink he should be gone.

'All right,' she agreed. 'But just one.'

They took their seats at the bar and ordered their drinks. When they came, they sat there for some time in silence, both absorbed in their own thoughts.

Finally, he turned to her. 'It's Kincaid, isn't it? The reason the evening fell flat.'

'No, of course not.'

'Oh, come on, Rachel. This is Sam you're talking to. You were fine until we ran into him. Admit it. You're still hung up on the guy, aren't you?' When she didn't answer, he went on, 'And he's obviously still hung up on you.'

She gave him a sharp look. 'What makes you think that?'

He threw back his head and laughed. 'If looks could kill I'd be a dead man. He was mad as hell at me. Jealous, I'd say.' He shook his head. 'I can't afford that, Rachel. I've got too much riding on his good will. I think you owe it to me to play it straight with me.'

She sighed. 'You're right. But I really wasn't lying. There was a short——' she paused, searching for the right word '—well, I guess you might call it a romantic interlude, a few weeks ago, but it didn't work out. We were working at cross purposes, and both agreed that a future together wasn't in the cards.'

He shook his red head again. 'Well, I'll take your word for it, but it sure didn't look that way to me. And I definitely do not want to get caught in the middle of a triangle. Not when the whole future of my business is at stake. If Kincaid pulled out now, I'd be dead in the water.'

'He won't,' she said firmly. 'Stephen may have his faults, but backing down on his word isn't one of them.'

'Well, OK,' he said warily. 'If you say so. I'll just have to take your word for it, I guess.'

*   *   *

For the rest of that night and all the next day, Rachel couldn't get her mind off Stephen. The unexpected encounter had shaken her more than she would have thought possible. She'd imagined, in her innocence, that she was over him for good, but all it took was one chance meeting and all the pain came flooding back to torment her.

She blamed Sam, in a way, for raising hopes she'd thought were dead. What had he seen in Stephen to make him believe he still cared for her? Whatever it was, it certainly escaped her. He hadn't called her, hadn't made any effort to see her. And this made her wonder how she would react if he did.

As it turned out, she soon got the chance to find out. The very next night he called her. In fact, the telephone was ringing as she stepped inside the house, and when she heard his voice she realised she'd been half expecting it.

'Hello, Rachel,' he said. 'It's Stephen.'

Just the sound of his voice still had the power to make her knees weak, and she sank down into the chair. 'Yes,' she said. 'I know.'

'Funny how we ran into each other last night.'

'Yes, it is.' There was a silence on the line.

'Overton looked quite presentable, for a change,' he remarked in an offhand tone. 'Did you have a good time?'

Then it came to her. He was jealous! A warm feeling of intense satisfaction stole over her. Stephen, jealous! That was one for the books! She'd always been the one tormented by suspicion, while he'd seemed proud of any attentions she received from other men, so sure of her love that apparently it never occurred to him that she'd look at anyone else twice.

Well, it wouldn't hurt him to know how it felt. 'Yes, we did. Actually, Sam's quite a good-looking man when he takes the trouble to pay some attention to his appearance. And, of course, we have a lot in common. Our work, you know.'

'I see,' he said stiffly. There was a long silence. 'Listen, Rachel,' he said at last, 'I've been wanting to talk to you. You know, about that last discussion we had. It's been on my mind for some time.'

He paused, obviously waiting for her to say something, but not only was she determined not to help him out, she hadn't a clue how to respond anyway. So she remained silent.

'Anyway,' he went on, 'I just want you to know how sorry I am about the misunderstanding between us. I never meant to hurt you, Rachel.' He paused again, then said, 'I was hoping we could still be friends.'

Rachel's mind raced. She knew quite well how much it cost a proud man like Stephen to humble himself that way, to call her and apologise, even to allow his jealousy of Sam to show. However, at the same time, she also knew that it didn't mean he'd changed his mind. He'd said he had no intention of marrying again, and he'd meant it. So what was the point of being 'friends'?

Then she suddenly remembered something Laura had said. If she loved him, she should fight for him. But how?

'Yes,' she said, temporising. 'I hope so too.'

'Then how about having dinner with me Saturday night?'

Well, there was her chance. What she'd do with it, she had no idea. She'd have to work that out later. What she did know was that she wasn't going to let it pass by.

'All right,' she said. 'I'd like that.'

'Good. I'll pick you up around seven.'

They said goodbye then, and after they'd hung up she sat there for a long time, thinking. Saturday! Today was Thursday. That gave her two days to make plans. But what plans?

As she got ready for bed that night, a favourite saying of her father's began to run through her head: 'You can catch more flies with honey than you can with vinegar'.

Maybe that was the answer.

After a sleepless, entirely fruitless night of pondering the problem, the minute her eyes opened the next morning she at least was quite certain about the first step.

As soon as she got to the office, she called to cancel all her afternoon appointments. She'd been working such long hours these past several weeks that she'd earned some time off. Sam was away consulting with a new printer in Redmond, and the new secretary could run the office quite well alone by now.

After a quick lunch at an outdoor espresso bar, she made tracks straight for the boutique where she'd run into Margaret that evening. Her favourite saleswoman was there to help her, and two hours later she walked out with the most luscious—and most wickedly expensive—dress she'd ever owned.

One amusing aftermath to the evening out with Sam was that he seemed to be avoiding her like the plague, speaking to her only when absolutely necessary, strictly on business matters, and then as briefly as possible.

She couldn't blame him. Since the chance encounter with Stephen at the Space Needle, Sam had it firmly in his head that Stephen was jealous of him, and who was she to criticise him for fearing to bite the hand that was feeding him? Besides, it was no great loss to her. She could never think of Sam as anything but a friend, even with his new clothes and haircut.

She assiduously avoided calling Laura during the next couple of days, knowing quite well that her sister would worm it out of her that she was going to see Stephen again. She'd really been very good about not raising the subject, but lately had been giving her looks that clearly indicated the dam would burst any moment and she wouldn't be able to stop herself from quizzing Rachel about the state of their relationship.

As luck would have it, however, Laura did call her late Saturday afternoon, just as Rachel was coming out of the shower, ostensibly to confirm that she'd be coming for the usual Sunday dinner with them the next day, but obviously bursting to find out what was going on, if anything, in the Stephen department.

'Er—how have you been?' she asked, after they'd settled their date for the next day.

'Oh, fine. Working hard.'

'Not too hard, I hope. You really ought to be having more fun at your age. You know—dances, parties, that kind of thing.'

Rachel laughed. 'Work *is* fun for me.'

There was a long silence. Then, 'Er—Rachel, I know I promised not to ask you about Stephen again——'

'Yes,' Rachel interrupted firmly. 'And you've been wonderful about that. I really appreciate it, Laura. Keep up the good work. Now I really have to go.'

'Aha!' Laura exploded at last. 'So something *is* going on! I knew it! Now, don't worry,' she added hurriedly before Rachel could protest. 'I'm not going to beat the subject to death. But I just want to say that if I'm right I couldn't be happier for you. Now, I'll let you go. See you tomorrow.'

With that, the connection was broken, and Rachel stood there with a dead telephone in her hands. Drat the woman! she thought as she replaced the receiver. Now she'd start manufacturing a grand romance that wasn't going to happen, and she'd have to go all through it again with her.

* * *

That evening at six-thirty, Rachel stood in front of her dressing-table mirror surveying the results of her preparations. The dress was perfect—a little wicked, but not blatantly seductive. The colour was wonderful: a pale green tissue-thin silk that brought out the highlights in her hazel eyes. It was a loose style, with a calf-length skirt, but the neckline plunged so low that she was tempted to pin it in place so that it wouldn't gape open when she bent over.

However, after practising with it for a couple of minutes, she decided against it. A pin would only spoil the lines. Besides, it was so well-cut and, although there was the hint of cleavage visible, her figure was not so voluptuous that she need worry. The gold high-heeled sandals set the dress off well, and thankfully there hadn't been a sign of rain all day. The finishing touch was her mother's emerald earrings, which complemented the green of the dress.

She'd debated having her hair done in a more sophisticated style, but, remembering how Stephen had always loved her hair hanging loosely to her shoulders, decided against it in the end. Thick and tawny, there was enough natural wave in it so that with just a little teasing it would stay in place.

She wore very little make-up. Her colour was naturally good, so that just a light sprinkling of neutral powder, a trace of pale green eyeshadow and a muted coral lipgloss were all she needed. She had, however, bought an outrageously expensive bottle of scent, and she applied it now behind her

ears and at her wrists—not too much, but just
enough to be noticeable.

Smoothing down the skirt of the green dress and
tucking a stray wisp of hair in place, she gave her
reflection one last careful examination. It wasn't
perfect, but she'd done the best she knew how.
Although there was artistry in her preparations,
she'd at least achieved the natural look she'd aimed
for.

Suddenly the doorbell rang. She put a hand to
her throat. Stephen! Prompt, as always. Her heart
started pounding so hard that she was certain he'd
be able to hear it. She took several deep breaths,
willing herself to be calm. A lot was at stake in this
one evening—her whole future riding on it—and
she didn't want to spoil it by succumbing to an
attack of nerves before it even began.

With a quick cursory glance in the mirror, she
switched off the light and went to answer the door,
forcing herself every step of the way to walk slowly.

When she opened it to him and saw him standing
there, tall and elegant, dressed impeccably, as
always, in a dark suit, a half-smile on his fine
mouth, all her nervousness fled, as if by magic. This
was Stephen, she reminded herself. How could
things go wrong when she was with him?

'Hello, Stephen,' she said with a smile. 'Come
on in. I'll just get my things.'

He stepped inside and closed the door behind
him, then stood there for a moment, his hands in
his trouser pockets, his grey eyes sweeping over her
appreciatively.

'You look very beautiful tonight,' he said softly. He bent over to kiss her lightly on the cheek. 'Mmm,' he said. 'And you smell good, too.'

'Thank you,' she replied. She turned and went to the hall cupboard for her coat. 'Shall we go?'

He took her to an expensive restaurant on the shores of Lake Union that specialised in fresh seafood. The dining-room was full, but the tables were set so far apart for the sake of the patrons' privacy that it didn't seem crowded. Stephen had obviously made a reservation, since they were conducted immediately to a choice table overlooking the lake.

The sun had just set, and it wasn't quite dark yet. The boats still out on the lake looked like ghostly shadows, their running lights twinkling in the dusky twilight. The dining-room itself was dimly lit, with a candle burning at each table, and in the background there was the low sound of tinkling glasses and muted conversation, punctuated occasionally by a subdued burst of laughter.

'This is very nice,' Rachel said after they'd ordered cocktails. 'I've never been here before.'

'Neither have I,' he replied. 'But I've heard excellent reports about it. Their speciality is halibut, by the way—one of your favourites, as I remember. I understand they prepare it in several interesting ways.'

'Oh, you know me,' she said with a light laugh. 'I like my meals pretty plain, especially fresh halibut.'

'So,' he said when their drinks arrived, 'how's the job?'

'Oh, it's great,' she replied eagerly. 'It's such a relief not to have to bother with bookkeeping and correspondence—and creditors—any more. Now I can spend all my time on editorial work. That's what I really love.' She smiled at him. 'Thanks to you, I might add. Or perhaps your rich company.'

'Oh, believe me, it wasn't charity,' he said immediately. 'Sam Overton may not possess the greatest head for business in the world, but he does have a reputation for excellent publishing expertise, and that's what we were looking for.'

'Well, he's in seventh heaven these days, and I don't think you'll regret your investment.' There was a short silence then while they sipped their drinks. 'And what about you?' she asked lightly. 'What plans are on your horizon these days, now that you've got Sam's company running so smoothly?'

He stared down at his glass for a moment, twirling it around slowly on the snowy linen tablecloth. 'Actually,' he said at last, looking up at her, 'I have no plans. Nothing definite, anyway.'

'Oh, I can hardly believe that,' she teased. 'You were never one to lie back and rest on your laurels. Surely there are several more worlds out there somewhere, waiting for you to come and conquer them?'

He cocked his head to one side and eyed her carefully. 'Do I detect a note of sarcasm in that remark?'

'Oh, no,' she assured him hurriedly. 'It's your life. I have nothing to say about it any more—that is, no personal stake in it. I just know you. When the next challenge comes along, you'll snap at it.'

'People change,' he said briefly. He picked up the enormous menu. 'Are you ready to order now?'

The rest of the evening passed in the same vein. They chatted pleasantly about their work, old friends they had in common, even the world situation. As time went on, Rachel felt more and more relaxed in his presence. He was wonderful company, and the appreciative glances he received from other women didn't hurt her ego. An attractive man was a social plus, no matter what their personal situation might be.

Perhaps they really could be friends! It was an odd thought, after all they'd been to each other in the past, but a promising one. Without the corrosive factor of possessiveness, she began to realise something that had never occurred to her before. She *liked* the man. In the past, their relationship had been so coloured by passion and, even more, by her own morbid jealousy that this simple fact had escaped her.

In her heart of hearts she was quite aware that she still loved him, still wanted him, and that friendship was a pale substitute for mutual desire. But it was better than suspicion and misunderstandings. He'd made it clear that she couldn't have him again in the way she really wanted him—as her husband—but she could learn to be satisfied with second best without rancour.

In fact, after dinner, while they sipped on liqueurs, she was perfectly happy to sit there in a contented silence, watching the few boats that were still out on the lake, the flashing lights of the traffic whizzing by high above on the Aurora Bridge. The evening had gone quite well, far better than she'd anticipated.

'Well,' he said, 'is there anything else you'd like to do this evening?'

She glanced at her watch. 'My goodness!' she said. 'It's almost eleven o'clock!'

He smiled. 'How time flies when you're having fun.' He reached across the table to put a hand over hers. 'At least, I hope you had a good time. Did you?'

'Oh, yes. I did. It was very pleasant.' She hesitated a moment, then plunged ahead. 'I'm so glad, Stephen, that we can be friends. All that bitterness I harboured for so long was eating me alive, and I didn't even know it.'

He nodded. 'I know.' That was all he said in response, but there was a light in his eyes that told her he was pleased. He pushed back his chair. 'Well, then, shall we go?'

They didn't have much to say on the way home. Rachel was still basking in the glow of the pleasant evening they'd spent together, and, as always, it seemed perfectly natural to be riding along next to Stephen, just like old times.

When they reached her house, he pulled up at the kerb, switched off the engine, and turned to her. 'Shall we go inside?'

For a moment she was taken aback and simply remained silent while she digested the unexpected question. 'I don't know, Stephen,' she said at last. 'I'm not sure that would be such a good idea.'

'I don't see why not,' he said, moving closer and bending his head towards her.

She pulled her head back and gave him a direct look. 'We decided to be friends,' she said evenly. 'Remember?'

He smiled. 'About that,' he murmured, reaching out for her. 'Friends kiss, don't they? And besides, I see no reason why we have to stick to the letter of the law.'

'I'm afraid we do, Stephen!' she said, twisting out of his grasp. 'And if we're going to remain friends, that's where it has to stop.'

'You don't really mean that,' he said.

The trouble was, she wasn't sure by now whether she did or didn't. It had certainly been her intention, but now the nearness of him, the scent of him, the dear face and well-loved body so close to her were doing strange things to her pulse-rate. While she hesitated, he reached out a hand to put it on her cheek, then slowly slid it downwards until it reached the loose opening of her dress.

Her head was in a whirl. Just the touch of his hand sent her blood coursing heatedly through her entire body. She didn't know what to do, what to say. She could only sit there as though paralysed. Then, when she felt his hand slip inside the opening of her dress, she suddenly came to her senses. Her head cleared; she knew exactly what she had to do, perhaps had unconsciously been planning to do from the minute she'd accepted the dinner date with him.

'No, Stephen!' she said huskily. She grabbed his hand and pushed it firmly away. 'It just won't do.'

'Why on earth not?' he asked in honest amazement.

'It just won't,' she stated flatly. 'That's not going to happen again. I agreed that we could be friends,' she explained patiently. 'I had a lovely time tonight and enjoyed every minute of it. But it's got to stop right there.'

He sat there frowning at her, his mouth twisted, his fingers drumming on the steering-wheel. In the glow of the street-light she could see that the expression on his face was one of complete bafflement, and she was amazed at how dense such an intelligent man could be when it came to grasping something he didn't want to understand.

Finally, he turned to her. 'And what about that weekend we spent together?' he asked in a low, intimate voice. 'Didn't that mean anything?'

She gave him a sharp look. The grey eyes were glittering at her, and the expression on his face now was one of such ineffable tenderness that she almost weakened again. A love for him so intense as to make her heart ache welled up in her. She wanted him. He wanted her. What would be the harm?

But it simply wasn't in her, and she shook her head sadly. 'It was wonderful,' she said. 'That's one area where we never did have a problem, isn't it? But it just wouldn't work for me. I'd be miserable in an affair where there was no future, no commitment, and I think you know that.'

He put his head in his hands and groaned. 'I don't understand you. You want me; you know damned good and well how badly I want you. We're responsible adults, not adolescents. There's no one else to consider and no one would be hurt. What could possibly be the harm in enjoying something we both want?'

'I already told you,' she said loftily. 'I just can't indulge in a meaningless affair.'

'Meaningless!' he shouted. 'How can you call something "meaningless" that was once so important to both of us?'

'But, Stephen, you said it yourself,' she said in a calm, sweetly reasonable tone. 'That's all over. And after thinking it over carefully, I've decided you're probably right. If any two people should have been able to make a success of marriage, it was us. We had everything going for us.'

'But we still do.'

She shook her head sadly. 'I don't think so. I don't blame you. Not any more. It was entirely my fault. You were right about my jealousy, not only of other women, but even of your success.'

He looked away. 'Well, I may have been overstating the case a little.'

'No. I don't think so. You were right, and I was wrong. I can see that now. In fact, I'm beginning to think I'm probably one of those women who shouldn't be married at all.'

'Ah, yes,' he said scornfully. 'Your precious career is much more important than a husband, a home, children.'

'Oh, I wouldn't say that. I'd love to have those things, but it's obviously not in the cards for me. I mean, I think now I've come to agree with your point of view on marriage. If you fail at it once, you don't deserve a second chance.'

He scowled darkly. 'I don't think I put it quite like that.'

She waved a hand in the air. 'Well, whatever. The idea is the same.'

She reached for the door and gave him one last sweet smile. 'Now, I'd really better go in. It's getting late. Thanks again for the lovely evening.'

'Wait a minute,' he snapped. 'Not so fast.'

She turned around to give him an enquiring look. 'Yes?'

His eyes were narrowed at her suspiciously. 'You're not by any chance trying to blackmail me into marriage, are you?'

She drew herself up and gave him a withering look. 'I don't think I deserve that, Stephen,' she said severely.

His gaze faltered. 'No. I guess not. I'm sorry. I apologise.' He thought a minute. 'Then it's Overton, isn't it?' he said in a flat tone.

She widened innocent eyes. 'Sam?' She laughed. 'What makes you think that?'

He shrugged. 'Well, why not? You said you had a lot in common.'

'At the moment,' she replied carefully, 'Sam and I are only friends. That's all I can say.'

He stared broodingly down at his hands for several seconds. 'Well,' he said at last, 'where does that leave us?'

She shrugged. 'I think it leaves us right where you said you wanted us to be—friends.'

'And that's as far as it goes?'

'I'm afraid so.'

'Well, we'll see about that.' He opened his door. 'Come on. I'll walk you to the house.'

After making sure she got inside all right, he muttered an abrupt goodnight, turned around, and stalked off down the path back to his car.

When he was gone, she closed the door and slumped back against it, her eyes closed tight. She didn't know whether she'd been very clever or just made the stupidest blunder of her whole life.

CHAPTER SEVEN

THE next morning Rachel awoke to a steady downpour, a phenomenon she was quite accustomed to as a Seattle native.

It was Sunday, and she'd been planning on working in the garden. Last week she'd noticed the slugs were out in force, chomping their way through the tender new shoots of the dahlias, but now, as she gazed out of the window at the rain slashing against the window-pane, the weather put paid to that plan.

She shrugged philosophically and slid out of bed. She'd brought home a manuscript she'd been meaning to read, and this would be as good a time as any to get at it. Not only had Sam been urging it on her for some time, but it would keep her mind off her constant preoccupation with Stephen.

After breakfast, she showered and got dressed in a comfortable old pair of blue denims and loose cotton shirt. Then she retrieved the manuscript from the table in the entry hall where she'd left it on Friday night and took it into the living-room to settle down in her favourite chair.

Stephen's chair! And this reminded her once again of last night. Actually, she supposed it had gone quite well. Although it bothered her that he'd accused her of trying to blackmail him into marriage, in the end she believed she'd convinced him that wasn't true. It certainly hadn't been her intention. All she'd really wanted, with the new dress, the expensive scent, the careful preparations, was to show him she could still be attractive.

Then, after he'd made his move and she'd stopped him cold, the picture had changed. He was the one who seemed to be promoting a closer, even a more committed relationship. She'd simply seized upon an opportunity he himself had offered her.

Was that blackmail? In the end she decided not to worry about it. She'd made her position clear, and she meant it. Since, according to him, any hope of marriage was out of the question, they'd have to be either friends or nothing. The ball was in his court now. She'd just have to wait and see what he did with it.

She opened the cover of the bound manuscript to the title page. *A Year at Sea*, she read, by Lars Helmerson. She frowned. Not a very catchy title, and sea stories could be excruciatingly boring, but Sam's policy, practically written in stone, was that they were committed to read every manuscript submitted to them on the basis that you never knew when a real winner would come along. His most cherished belief was that the history of publishing was full of cases where a great book had been passed up simply by not giving it a thorough reading before rejecting it.

She sighed, turned the page, and started in on chapter one.

*   *   *

When she finally tore her bleary eyes away from the manuscript, she blinked several times to clear her vision, then glanced at her watch. It was past two o'clock in the afternoon! She'd spent a solid four hours reading.

The book that had looked so unpromising at first glance had turned out to be one of the most fascinating stories she'd ever read, even granting her lack of interest in sea sagas. Although the author had recounted several harrowing adventures sailing alone across the Pacific, it was far, far more than that. The man had obviously lived a largely solitary life, a long life, a deeply thoughtful life, and the insights he had gleaned about human nature, man's place in the universe, the meaning of human existence were astounding to her—and fascinating.

With just a few revisions and deletions of repetitive passages, and a new title, she knew they had a real winner. There was no mistaking that inner glow she'd come to recognise as her editorial instinct telling her she'd come across a real gem.

Just then she heard the distant ringing of the telephone, barely audible in the quiet house, since she always muffled the bell when she was reading so as not to disturb her concentration. She wasn't quite through with the manuscript yet, but her growling stomach told her it was time for lunch anyway.

She got up out of the chair, stretched her cramped muscles, and went to answer it. On the way she could see that it had stopped raining outside and a pale sun was struggling to break through the clouds.

'Hello, Rachel,' came Stephen's voice. 'How are you this afternoon?'

The sound of his voice filled her with a warm glow, but she quickly damped it down. 'I'm fine,' she said. 'How are you?'

'As well as can be expected after the way you treated me last night. I'm still shivering from that cold shoulder.' But before she could object to his phraseology, he went on quickly. 'I tried to call you several times today, but I guess you were gone.'

'No, I was right here. I just didn't hear the telephone. I've been absorbed in a wonderful new manuscript. It's a sea story, and makes fascinating reading.'

'I thought you couldn't stand sea stories.'

She laughed. 'Ordinarily I can't, but this one is different. It's hard to explain. The man who wrote it is obviously an old salt who has lived a long, interesting life, and has set down his experiences in a really compelling style.'

'Well, do you think you can tear yourself away from it long enough to take a drive with me this afternoon? It's stopped raining. I thought we might hop on the Kingston ferry and go up to Deception Pass. How about it?'

'Oh, Stephen, I'm sorry. I can't. I always have dinner with Laura and John on Sunday.'

'Surely they'd understand?'

Rachel's mind raced. She wanted to see him, to be with him. But was it wise? Knowing him, he most likely had a brand new plan for seduction all mapped out. Besides, she really was already committed to go to Laura's, and it wouldn't hurt Stephen to realise she wasn't always going to be there at his beck and call. She had nothing to lose, after all.

'I'm not sure that would be such a good idea,' she said slowly at last.

'Listen, I just want to see you, Rachel. No strings. Surely we can afford simply to spend a pleasant afternoon together?'

Rachel could feel herself weakening. Quite simply, she wanted to go with him. As for Laura, not only would she understand her backing out of the dinner at the last minute, she'd positively push her into doing so once she found out it was Stephen she was going with. And it would only take a few probing questions to get that information out of her.

'All right,' she said at last. 'Give me an hour.'

'Good. I'll be there some time around three o'clock.'

After a late lunch at a waterfront restaurant in the small town of Edmonds, they took the Kingston ferry over to Whidbey Island and drove up the narrow, wooded road to the bridge over Deception Pass.

It had been such a lovely, relaxed afternoon, just like old times: laughing at the same jokes, noticing the same things in the passing scenery, even enjoying the same music on the car radio.

Even the weather held beautifully, and it wasn't until they were on their way back to the city, relaxed and pleasantly tired, that Rachel began to wonder if there would be a reprise of last night's scene. And if so, what she'd do about it.

As they took the exit off the motorway to get to her house, she suddenly realised her plan was backfiring badly. She knew darned well that when he did try to end such a perfect day with another attempt at lovemaking she wouldn't have the strength to refuse him.

When they arrived at her house, he parked in front, switched off the engine, then turned to her. 'I'll just see you to the door,' he said. 'Then I'd better let you get on with your work.'

For a second she was too stunned to say anything and simply sat there gaping at him. It was the last thing she'd expected. Recovering herself, she quickly looked away, hoping he hadn't noticed her reaction to his blunt dismissal.

'Oh, don't bother getting out,' she said, opening her door. She stepped out on to the pavement and bent over to speak to him through the open window. 'Thanks for the drive—and the lunch,' she said with a forced smile.

He nodded. 'My pleasure.'

She hurried up the path and let herself inside the house. Before closing the door, she turned around to wave at him, but by then he'd already driven off.

She spent the rest of the evening trying to concentrate on the Helmerson manuscript, but, for some reason, what had seemed so fascinating to her just that morning now came across as a mere jumble of words she could make no sense of.

Finally, she gave up in disgust and went to soak in a hot tub. As she lay there, her head back, her eyes closed, the first image that sprang to her mind was of Stephen. She knew she should be grateful to him for taking her at her word, should be pleased that he'd honoured her decision just to be friends, with no passion. She'd won, after all, and got what she wanted.

Then why did she feel so let down?

The next morning, when she arrived at the office, Sam was already there, an unusual phenomenon these days when he seemed to be doing everything in his power to avoid her. He was deep in conversation with another man, both of them with their backs turned to her.

When he heard her come in, he turned around. 'Ah, Rachel,' he said, beaming. 'There's someone here I want you to meet.' He turned to the other man. 'This is Lars Helmerson, the writer whose book I've been raving about. I hope you've had a chance to read it. Lars, this is Rachel Spencer, my star editor.'

Rachel could only stare. She'd built up a picture in her mind of the author of the manuscript she'd read over the weekend as a tough old sea-salt, grizzled and weather-beaten, certainly at least in middle age.

What she saw was a tall, strapping Nordic giant of a man, with a thick head of shaggy blond hair, cut rather long, and surely only in his early twenties, with a smooth face and high, youthful colour. Although he was dressed casually, in well-worn jeans and dark blue jersey, there was an air of experience about him that belied his years. He was gazing at her now with a pair of the most startlingly blue eyes she'd ever seen.

Collecting herself, she walked over to him and held out her hand. 'Mr Helmerson,' she said with a smile. 'It's a pleasure to meet you.'

He returned the smile, revealing a mouthful of even white teeth. 'Lars, please,' he said, grasping her hand in one enormous, calloused paw. 'So you're an editor,' he went on. 'I've always wanted to meet one.'

'We're quite human,' she said with a little laugh. She withdrew her hand and glanced over at Sam. 'I did have a chance to read the manuscript over the weekend, and was most impressed with it.'

'Ah,' Sam said. 'I knew you would be.'

She turned back to the blond giant. 'Of course you need to understand, Lars, it still needs some work to get it in shape for publication.'

His face fell. 'A lot of work?' he asked warily. 'I don't think I could face rewriting the thing again.'

She shook her head. 'No, not a lot of work. Just a little polishing, possibly cutting out a few passages. It certainly won't mean rewriting the whole thing. It's almost perfect as it stands. And don't worry. That's what I'm for, to help you make those decisions.'

He gave her a long, appreciative look, almost as though she were a doctor who had just told him he'd live after all. 'Well, that's a relief.' He reached up a hand and ran it over the thick, unruly thatch of hair. 'This is all new to me, you know. I need all the guidance I can get.'

'Oh, Rachel's great at that kind of thing,' Sam put in excitedly. 'You two will work very closely together over—how long would you say, Rachel, it'll take to get it in shape to publish?'

She shrugged. 'I'll have to give it a more careful reading before I can answer that. Say, two weeks to a month, depending on how hard Lars is willing to work.'

'What I had in mind,' Sam said, 'was to get the galleys set and printed out as soon as possible, then start submitting to paperback publishers at the same time as we bring it out in hardback. How does that sound to you?'

'Well, it can't hurt to test the waters and see what kind of offers we get for it.'

'I'll handle that end of it,' Sam said. 'You concentrate on working with Lars to get it in final form as quickly as possible.'

Rachel smiled at Lars. 'Well, we've got our orders. Might as well get to work right away. Come on into my office and we'll see if we can at least make a start. I do have a few things in mind already, just from a first reading. We can start there.'

Although the next few days were taken up almost entirely by consultations with Lars Helmerson,

Rachel's mind constantly strayed to thoughts of Stephen and his odd behaviour on Sunday. It wasn't like him to give up so easily, and she had to wonder if he'd changed his mind about her. Perhaps that was even his idea of a farewell scene.

Then on Wednesday night he called her at home. 'I have two tickets to *Les Misérables* for Friday night,' he said. 'Would you care to go with me?'

'Oh, yes,' she replied. 'I'd love to. From all I've heard, it's wonderful.'

'Good. It starts at eight o'clock. I'll pick you up around seven-fifteen. Give us plenty of time to park.'

Well, she thought, as she hung up, what would be the harm? From his behaviour on Sunday, he seemed to be as anxious as she was to keep their relationship on an impersonal level. After all, they were old friends. It might just work.

The only problem was that in the end her own feelings betrayed her. Sitting next to him in the theatre on Friday night, discussing their enjoyment of the brilliant musical at the interval, then, later, having a drink at the cocktail lounge across the street while the traffic thinned out all set up an aching feeling in her bones and blood for something far more than mere friendship.

At one point during the performance, helpless with muffled laughter at the clever patter in the barroom scene, she turned to him and reached out, clutching at his arm. Their eyes met, and she saw that he was having as much trouble holding in his own merriment. But he made no effort to take the hand on his sleeve or touch her in any way. Quickly she withdrew it and turned her eyes back to the stage.

When he took her home, the same pattern as Sunday was repeated, except that this time he insisted on seeing her to the door. After she'd unlocked it, she turned back to thank him again, half hoping, half fearing he'd ask to come in. In fact, it was on the tip of her tongue to invite him. What could be a more perfect ending to such a pleasant evening?

But before she got the chance, he'd said a brusque goodnight, turned from her, and was striding purposefully down the path, almost as though he was afraid she *would* invite him in.

What's wrong with me? she asked herself as she locked and bolted the door. She'd made the rules. She'd just have to abide by them.

During the next few weeks they saw each other fairly regularly—almost every other night, in fact—and each time was the same as the last. They'd go out to dinner or to a show, have a good time together, enjoy each other's company, then he'd drive her home and leave her at the door without asking to come in or so much as a friendly peck on the cheek.

In fact, he seemed to be going out of his way not to touch her at all, even when seating her at a restaurant or helping her on or off with her coat, and by now she was becoming so frustrated that she had to make a resolute effort to restrain herself from making the first move herself towards a more intimate relationship. She kept reminding herself that, however unfulfilling the situation was, she was the one who had created it. But that was cold comfort when night after night he simply left her at the door.

The one thing that saved her from making a total fool of herself over him was the long hours she was spending with Lars, getting his book in shape. Sam had managed to interest three paperback publishers in it, and had now given her a deadline. It only gave them a few weeks.

To her delight, it was coming along quite well. Lars was an apt pupil, and although he did his share of groaning over each change she wanted made he always did it, and even admitted her suggestions were improving the quality of the book tremendously.

One thing about their close collaboration did trouble her, however. As the days passed, they naturally saw a lot of each other. He'd even started coming to her house in the evenings and at the weekend, so they could get the revisions finished as quickly as possible. Little by little it began to dawn on her that he was giving her some strange looks, almost calf-eyed, the brilliant blue gaze following her around the room, fixed upon her when she was sitting next to him.

She kept telling herself it couldn't be. He had to be at least five years younger than she was! If his mind was running in that direction, it was probably just because she was filling a much-needed role for him, as mentor, guide, even doctor for his book.

*   *   *

It was early June now, and one Friday afternoon Stephen called her at work to ask her out to dinner.

'Oh, I'm sorry, I can't,' she replied. 'I've already made plans to work with Lars this evening on his book. Can't we make it some other time? Tomorrow night, perhaps?'

'Sorry,' he said curtly. 'I'm going out of town tomorrow.'

'Oh? Where are you going?' She could have bitten her tongue out the moment the words were spoken. She had no right to check up on him, nor did she want him to think that was what she was doing. 'Oh, never mind,' she added quickly. 'It's none of my business.'

'Well, I have to fly to New York, then on to London to wind up a few things there.' He hesitated for a moment, then went on, 'I'll be gone for at least two weeks, and I'd really like to see you before I go.'

Her first thought was to wonder if he was taking anyone with him. She actually knew nothing about his personal life, or what he did on the nights he wasn't with her. It occurred to her for the first time that a passionate man like Stephen surely wouldn't put up with a celibate life for long. It could even be that the reason he was accepting her stupid friendship rule so graciously was that he was finding satisfaction somewhere else.

At the mere thought of Stephen in another woman's arms, a red-hot wave of sheer jealousy swept through her. It was time to put an end to this impasse, and it looked as though she'd have to be the one to do it.

Besides, Lars really was becoming too demanding of her time, too dependent on her. It wouldn't hurt him to plug along on his own for a while. She'd spelled out pretty clearly the passage she wanted changed. He could do it just as well without her.

'All right,' she said at last. 'I'll put off the session with Lars.'

'Good,' he replied promptly. 'Anywhere special you'd like to have dinner?'

'I'll tell you what,' she said. 'So far you've done all the entertaining. Why don't I cook dinner for you?'

'Sounds great. It's been a long time since I've had anything but restaurant food.'

She glanced at her watch. It was just past three o'clock. 'How busy are you at the moment?' she asked.

'Nothing I can't put off. Why?'

'How would you like to meet me at the public market and help me with the shopping for dinner?' She laughed. 'I'm afraid my cupboards are bare.'

'That sounds like a good idea,' he replied. 'What time?'

'Give me an hour to get things cleared away here and call Lars to tell him our meeting is off. Say, four o'clock. That way we'll just beat the commuter traffic.'

*   *   *

The Pike Place Market was located in the heart of the city on the waterfront, not far from the busy ferry terminal. It was a fine, sunny day, and just like old times to shop there with Stephen again. They wandered leisurely along the wide aisles, crammed with tourists at this time of year, listening to the produce vendors at their stalls calling attention to the superior quality of their wares, watching the fishmongers displaying their fresh catch, breathing in the familiar smell of fresh bakery goods, rotting produce and salt water.

After a careful examination of everything offered, traversing one end of the huge building to the other, they finally settled on fresh halibut, crisp lettuce, crusty French bread and some raw tortellini from the Italian market across from the bakery.

By the time they'd carried their purchases to Stephen's car, it was almost five o'clock.

'I'm afraid we didn't miss the commuter traffic after all,' Rachel said, as Stephen started the car.

'Oh, we'll manage,' he replied with a smile.

There was finally a brief lull in the steady stream of oncoming traffic, and he slid swiftly out of the parking space on to the street. It was stop and go the whole way, but, since she didn't live far from town, and they stayed off the clogged inter-state, it only took about twenty minutes to get to her house.

Although Rachel had insisted on paying for the groceries herself, Stephen had stopped at the liquor store to pick up a bottle of wine produced at a local

winery, some fine French cognac and the makings
for vodka martinis.

When he unpacked the bottles and set them on
the kitchen counter, she had to laugh. 'Stephen!'
she cried. 'What in the world were you thinking
of? We'll never begin to drink all that!'

'Well, I didn't really expect we would,' he replied. He crossed over to put the wine in the re-
frigerator. 'We can save what's left for another
time, though, can't we?' He came back to her. 'If
we're going to cook the halibut outdoors, I'd better
get the fire going in the barbecue.'

'Good idea,' she replied. 'The grill is still out on
the patio under a plastic cover.' She reached in one
of the sacks and pulled out a bag of charcoal
briquets. 'Here,' she said, handing it to him. 'The
fire-starter is on top of the grill.'

He opened the sliding glass door to the patio and
went outside. As Rachel put the groceries away, she
began to hum under her breath. It seemed so
natural, and so right, to be pottering around the
kitchen with Stephen again, just like a replay of
domestic scenes from the past.

Every once in a while, as she worked, she would
glance outside to watch him as he took the cover
off the barbecue, undid the bag of briquets, took
off the metal grill, poured the charcoal on the
bottom bed—all the homely little chores he used to
do.

He was dressed casually in dark trousers and a
grey knit shirt that just matched the colour of his
eyes. He looked as though he needed a haircut, the

thick dark hair at the back of his neck curling just a little. Every move he made, every gesture was so familiar to her, and so endearing.

In a few minutes he came back inside. 'I've been wondering,' he said. 'Did you happen to keep my old camera? I thought if it was still around I might take it to London with me.'

She was at the kitchen counter, breaking up the lettuce for the salad, and turned around to give him an incredulous look. 'Do you mean to say a photography buff like you has gone for two years without a camera?'

'No, but that old one has always been my favourite. None of the newer models can quite measure up to it. But maybe you have a use for it yourself?'

'Oh, no. I never could take proper pictures. Somehow I always managed to cut the top of someone's head off, or miss just the scenic spot I intended to shoot. Be my guest. It should still be in the bottom drawer of the sideboard in the dining-room.'

'I'll just go and have a look for it, then.'

While he was gone, she finished up the lettuce and sliced the tomatoes, then put a plastic cover on the bowl. There really wasn't much else to do except for cooking the pasta at the last minute. She could put the water on the stove to boil when Stephen started barbecuing the halibut.

Just as she was setting the salad bowl in the fridge, she heard him coming back. 'Did you find it?' she called.

When he didn't answer her right away, she turned around to see him walking slowly towards her, carrying something that was definitely not a camera, his head bent, totally absorbed.

Instantly she recognised the album of wedding pictures. She'd completely forgotten they were in the same drawer as the camera.

Finally he looked up at her. 'See what I found,' he said, holding it up.

Their eyes met and held for a long moment. Then he smiled, went over to the kitchen table, and set the album down on top. He stood there, leafing through it, while she watched him, the expression on his face as he came to each photograph sometimes frowning, sometimes smiling, and at one point bursting out into a sudden gust of loud laughter.

'Will you come and look at this?' he called to her.

She went to his side and leaned over his shoulder, gazing down at the picture he was pointing at. It was a candid shot of the car they'd driven off in after the wedding. Stephen's friends had sprayed messages all over it in white paint and tied a long string of tin cans to the rear bumper.

He turned to her. 'It took me an hour to wash off all that paint and get rid of the junk,' he said. 'Remember? You made me stop at the first service station we came to. Refused to arrive at the hotel looking like newly-weds.'

'Oh, yes. How could I forget? For all the good it did me,' she added in a wry tone. 'If you recall, when I got out of the car in front of the hotel, a pile of rice fell out of my clothes. And right at the feet of the bell-boy, to boot.'

Smiling, their eyes met again and became locked together. Then gradually the smiles faded. Rachel could feel the warmth in her bloodstream, the quickening of her pulse, and knew he felt it too. Throwing caution to the winds, all her resistance to him drained away. Quite simply, she wanted this man, on any terms, any way she could get him.

He rose slowly from his chair and stood before her, his eyes never leaving hers. 'There's something I want to ask you,' he said at last in a low voice.

Her heart was pounding crazily. 'Yes? What is it?'

'Come to London with me.'

CHAPTER EIGHT

RACHEL'S heart soared. A trip to London with Stephen! It sounded like heaven. And he wasn't going with anyone else, as she'd feared. She was just about to tell him that of course she'd go with him, when she remembered Lars and his book and came back to reality with a dull thud. She couldn't go off in the middle of that project. It wouldn't be fair to Lars or Sam. Too much was riding on it.

'Oh, Stephen, I can't,' she said, turning away from him in sheer despair.

He put a hand on her shoulder. 'Why not? I've behaved myself, haven't I? Kept my distance, played it your way entirely. You know how badly I still want you, and you can't tell me you don't want me. What does it take, Rachel, to get past those defences of yours?'

She turned back then to face him. 'It's not that, Stephen. At least, not entirely. I just can't leave now, not until this book I'm working on is ready for publication.'

'It's that damned writer, then, isn't it?'

'No, not in that way. But we are at a crucial stage in revising his book, and I just can't leave him now.'

'Can't someone else do that?' He placed his hand on her face and gazed down at her, the grey eyes glinting softly. 'We could have a wonderful time together. Two weeks, away from everyone, in one of the most interesting cities in the world. Come on, Rachel, say you'll come with me.'

His head was bending lower. In a minute he'd kiss her. She wanted him to kiss her. What was more, she had a feeling she'd end up weakening and going with him to London. After all, which was more important—Lars Helmerson's book or her own future?

She closed her eyes. Her lips parted, and she stood there motionless, waiting in excited anticipation for the longed-for touch of his mouth on hers.

Just then the telephone on the counter shrilled piercingly, breaking into the dead silence of the room. Rachel jumped and her eyes flew open as Stephen's hand fell from her face. He was scowling darkly at her.

'Don't answer that,' he said.

'Oh, Stephen, I have to. It might be important.'

'More important than what we're doing?' he asked in a tight voice.

'Well, no, but...'

'Go on, then,' he said with a wave of his hand. 'Answer it.'

She hesitated, but as the persistent ring continued it began to get on her nerves, and she knew she had to do something. She ran to the counter and snatched it up.

'Yes,' she said curtly.

'Rachel, it's Lars.'

She sighed. 'Yes, Lars, what is it? I'm very busy at the moment.'

'I've got to see you,' he went on in a rush. 'I'm stuck. I can't do it. Not alone.'

There was real panic in his voice, and Rachel's heart sank. She'd been afraid of this. He'd become so dependent on her that he was losing confidence in himself.

'Of course you can, Lars,' she said in a soothing tone. 'You wrote the book in the first place, after all, without any help from me.'

'That was different. I feel totally paralysed. I've got to see you. I can be there in ten minutes.'

'No!' she said firmly. 'You can't do that. I told you. I'm busy.'

There was a long silence. 'All right, then,' he said at last in tones of deepest despair. 'I've had it. If you won't help me, then I'll just burn the damn thing and take off in my boat. I don't know what made me think I was a writer in the first place.'

'But you *are* a writer, Lars.'

'Not without you, I'm not.'

Rachel's mind raced. There was no way out of it. She had no alternative. She'd have to make Stephen understand. She couldn't go to London with him in any case. Their unfinished business would just have to wait until he got back.

'All right, Lars,' she said at last. 'Come on over.'

She hung up then, and turned to explain to Stephen what had happened. He was standing by the table where she'd left him, his arms crossed over his chest, looking like thunder, his mouth set in a grim line, his grey eyes stormy.

She started to speak, but he held up a hand to stop her. Then he put his hands in his trouser pockets and came walking slowly towards her.

'It seems you've made your decision about going to London with me,' he stated flatly.

'Stephen, please try to understand. I have to help him. If I don't there's no telling what he'll do.'

'Fine,' he said. 'Then I'd better get out of here so you can work undisturbed.'

He turned from her and started walking slowly away towards the door, almost as though he was hoping she'd stop him. She stood there staring after him for a few seconds. She couldn't let him just vanish again. But what could she say?

'Stephen,' she called.

He stopped, stood motionless for a few moments, then turned slowly around. 'Yes?'

'Please stay a while. He won't be here for another half-hour.' She faltered and raised a hand helplessly in the air. 'We need to talk. I don't want you to leave like this.'

'Why?' he said with a thin smile. 'What's the point?'

She searched her mind. 'Well, what about our dinner?'

He muttered something unprintable about the dinner, then stalked off. The front door opened and closed. Then she heard his car start up out in front, the squeal of tyres as he drove away.

The album was still lying on the kitchen table where he'd left it. Slowly she walked over and stared down at the photograph of their getaway car for a moment. Then she closed the cover.

The next week was so hectic that she didn't have time to brood over what had happened. She spent ten-hour days soothing and coddling the frantic Lars, so that all she could do was fall into bed each night exhausted.

She didn't hear from Stephen, nor did she expect to. He'd be gone another week. By then the book would be ready for publication and she'd at least get Lars off her hands. If Stephen didn't call her when he got back, she'd track him down and make him listen to her. He still wanted her—that much was clear—or he wouldn't have asked her to go to London with him in the first place, or been so angry when it turned out she couldn't.

There was another reason for her growing sense of urgency, far more pressing then either Stephen's or her own egoistic needs and desires.

For some time the vague, hardly conscious suspicion had been growing in her mind that she might be pregnant. Her cycle had always been wildly erratic, so at first she'd simply dismissed it as a normal phenomenon. But as time passed, and other symptoms appeared—a slight tenderness in her breasts, a touch of morning nausea—she had to face it as a real possibility.

If she really was pregnant, didn't she owe it to herself, and to her unborn child, to rise above her pride and do everything in her power to win its father back? When he did return from London, she'd tell him of her suspicions. It might make all the difference. He'd always wanted children.

That Sunday was to be the last working day before the deadline. She and Lars had worked at her house practically non-stop all day Saturday, drinking cup after cup of strong coffee, the telephone turned off, not quitting until midnight, when he had finally staggered back to his boat, bleary-eyed and exhausted.

They'd started up again early this morning, working through the entire day. Finally, by six o'clock, they were finished.

'There,' she said, turning over the last page and closing the cover. 'We're done. If you'll just tighten up that last paragraph as I suggested, it'll make a really solid ending.'

'Well, thank God,' Lars said with deep feeling. 'I never thought we'd get to the end of it.' He pushed his chair back, rose to his feet, and stretched widely. Then he bent down to brace his hands flat on the table and leaned towards her, smiling broadly. 'I think we deserve a celebration.'

'Right,' she said, jumping to her feet. 'I believe I have a bottle of brandy tucked away in the top shelf. I'll just go and look.'

As she passed by him on her way to the cupboard, he reached out and took her by the arm. 'That wasn't what I had in mind,' he said. 'I meant we should do something really exciting.'

She laughed. 'Like what?'

'Oh, I don't know,' he said with a shrug. His hold on her arm tightened. 'I know what I'd like.'

Rachel stiffened. She'd been a little afraid of this all along. Now that their work together was finished, she'd assumed it would just go away, but apparently the blond giant had other ideas.

With another nervous little laugh, she pulled her arm out of his grasp and moved a few steps away from him. 'What's that?' she asked lightly.

He took the step that separated them and put his hands on her shoulders, gazing down at her out of those incredibly blue eyes. 'I want you to come with me to my boat,' he said in a low voice.

'You mean, go out sailing some afternoon?' she asked, puzzled.

'No, that's not what I mean. Listen,' he went on in a low, urgent tone. 'If you and Sam are right about the book, I could make a lot of money from it. We could go anywhere together. Tahiti, Samoa, Tasmania. There's a whole world out there I'd like to show you. Come with me, Rachel.'

She could only stare up at him, open-mouthed. He was serious! Dead serious. She was so stunned that she didn't know what to say, even what to think.

The next thing she knew, his huge arms had come around her and he was pulling her up tightly against him. Before she could twist her head away, he was kissing her. The shock brought her to her senses at last and under the punishing pressure of his mouth on hers she tried to cry out, to disentangle herself from his powerful grip.

Just then she heard a loud cough coming from behind Lars, and another voice rang out. 'I hope I'm not interrupting anything important.'

Her head swivelled around. It was Stephen! He was standing just inside the door, leaning against the sill, his arms crossed in front of him, a grim look on his sombre face. Lars released her immediately.

'Stephen!' she cried, putting a hand to her throat. 'What are you doing here?'

'The door was open,' he said. 'I've been trying to call you since yesterday, but no one answered. When I called Laura this morning, she said she'd been trying to get you, too, and was getting worried about you, so I said I'd come over to see if you were all right.'

'I'm sorry,' she stammered. 'We've been working all weekend, and I pulled the plug on the telephone so we wouldn't be interrupted. Anyway,' she went on hurriedly, 'I thought you were still in London.'

His eyes flicked over to Lars, who was standing there looking like a hound about to be beaten, then back to Rachel. 'Obviously,' he said in a decidedly nasty tone. 'I came back a week early.'

'I see,' she stammered. He was *very* angry. Somehow she'd have to make him see that it wasn't what he thought. She turned to Lars. 'Er—Stephen, this is Lars Helmerson, the writer I've been working with. Lars, this is Stephen Kincaid.'

The two men stood there glaring at each other, neither of them making a move to shake hands. Rachel knew she had to do something to defuse the explosive situation. Any moment now she was afraid the two men would start prowling around each other like two wolves defending their territory.

She turned to Lars. 'Lars, we've finished up here,' she said in a firm voice that brooked no contradiction. 'So I think you'd better go now.'

The blond giant opened his mouth as though to argue with her, but at the look on her face obviously decided not to. He stood there scowling, undecided, for a moment, then finally, without another word, turned and left.

The minute he was gone, Stephen turned on Rachel with fire flashing in the grey eyes. He gazed at her for a second or two, his thin mouth curled, a look of utter contempt etched on every feature.

'Well, Rachel,' he said at last. 'I never would have thought it of you.'

'What do you mean? I know it looks bad, but it isn't what you think. I can explain——'

Ignoring her words completely, he went on in the same flat, accusing tone. 'I thought you had higher standards than to indulge in a cheap fly-by-night affair. And with a mere boy, at that!'

By now she was growing angry herself at the high moral tone he was taking. 'Isn't that a little like the pot calling the kettle black?' she enquired archly.

'I haven't the slightest idea what you're talking about,' he stated flatly.

'Well, now you know how it feels!' she cried, frustrated beyond endurance by his pig-headed refusal to believe her. 'How I felt the night I found you and Margaret in exactly the same situation. You were quick enough to defend yourself then.'

His eyes flew open at that and for a moment he had nothing to say. 'All right,' he muttered grudgingly at last. 'You may have a point. If so, then *you* know how it feels to be blamed for something you didn't do. The shoe is on the other foot now, isn't it? If it pinches a little, you have only yourself to blame.'

'No!' she cried. 'It's not the same thing at all. I don't see what right you have to judge me, especially not by comparing my perfectly innocent relationship with Lars Helmerson to what happened between you and Margaret.'

He crossed over to her in three long strides and pushed his face up close to hers. 'Just how innocent can it be when I come here and find you making love in the kitchen, of all places? It was quite clear then why you chose to stay here with him rather than go to London with me.'

'We were *not* making love!' she exclaimed hotly. 'And I didn't choose to stay here. It was a commitment, an obligation.' She shook her head. 'Oh, what's the use? Think what you like.'

'I intend to,' he stated flatly.

'I don't know why I'm bothering to explain, anyway. After all, Stephen, you don't want me. You made that clear. If someone else does, I don't see that you have any right to complain.'

Speechless with anger by now, he took a men-
acing step towards her. For a moment she was
positive he'd strike her, but instead he opened his
mouth, snapped it shut, then turned around and
stalked out of the room, out of the house, and, she
was certain, this time out of her life for good.

It was Laura who finally noticed something was
wrong and pushed her into seeing a doctor. It was
the Sunday afternoon following Stephen's surprise
visit. They were sitting out in the back garden of
Laura's house. John had taken the children to the
science fair at the Seattle Centre, and the two sisters
were having a scratch meal of Saturday night left-
overs.

'I thought you liked lasagne,' Laura commented.

'Oh, I do,' Rachel replied hastily.

'Then why are you pushing it around your plate
instead of eating it?' Laura sighed. 'I thought you'd
be grateful if I spared you one of my cooking ex-
periments today and just gave you one of the old
stand-bys.'

Rachel pushed her plate away. 'I'm sorry, Laura.
I don't feel very hungry for some reason.'

'Yes, I've noticed you haven't had much appetite
lately.' She gave her a closer look. 'You're not sick,
are you?'

Rachel forced out a weak smile. 'Not really. Just
a little tired.'

Laura settled back in her chair. 'It's Stephen, isn't
it?'

'Oh, I suppose. At least partly. That and finishing the work on the Helmerson book. I always feel a let-down when a major project like that is finally over.'

'Have you heard from him at all?'

'Who, Lars?'

'No! Of course not! Who cares about Lars? You know quite well who I mean.'

Rachel shook her head. 'No, not a word. And I don't expect to. He was furious when he found me with Lars that day he came back from London. Wouldn't even listen to me. Finally, I just gave up trying to explain.'

'Well, I hate to bring this up, but that's pretty much what happened when you found him with Margaret Fulton, isn't it?' She braced herself visibly for the onslaught of bad temper she clearly expected.

But Rachel only gave her a wan smile. 'Yes, I guess it is. That's what Stephen said, too.'

'Now I know there's something really wrong with you,' Laura said sharply. 'Ordinarily you'd snap my head off for a comment like that.' She leaned across the table and gave her a long, searching look. 'You know, you really do look terrible. You've got circles under your eyes; you look as though you've been losing weight.' Then she laughed. 'All except in the bosom department. I must say something is filling out ...' Then she stopped, clapped her hand over her mouth, and stared at her sister with something like horror in her eyes.

Rachel flushed deeply and started to rise from her chair. 'I am feeling kind of drained out these days, Laura,' she said. 'In fact, if you don't mind, I think I'll run along home now.'

'Sit down, Rachel!' Laura commanded sternly. Too tired to argue, Rachel sank slowly back down in her chair. 'You're pregnant, aren't you?' she asked quietly after a moment.

Rachel gave her one miserable look. 'I don't know. I think maybe I am.'

'You haven't seen a doctor?' Rachel shook her head. 'Well, that's the first step. No point getting into a panic before you're sure. Although I must say you have all the classic symptoms.' She hesitated for a moment. 'Does Stephen know?'

Rachel shrugged. 'What's to know? I'm not even sure myself.' She got up from her chair again. 'Now I really must go.'

'All right,' Laura said, rising to her feet. She crossed over to her sister and put an arm around her shoulders. 'Just promise me you'll see a doctor right away. Believe me, you'll feel better once you know for sure. And remember, honey, I'm on your side. John and I will do everything we can to help you, no matter what it is.'

'Thanks, sis,' she said. 'Now, I'd better get out of here before I start to cry. That's another thing. I seem to feel constantly on the verge of tears these days.'

'Don't worry about it. It's only another symptom.'

* * *

Three days later, Rachel staggered out of her doctor's office in a daze, clutching a handful of sample vitamins, prescriptions for nausea and calcium tablets and a booklet with diet and exercises for expectant mothers.

She'd been practically certain before she saw the doctor, had even become almost used to the idea, especially after her talk with Laura. But now, somehow, having it officially confirmed made it much worse. What in the world was she going to do?

She placed a tentative hand on her still flat stomach. A baby! A child of her own! Stephen's child, too. Her eyes grew suddenly misty at the thought. Her doctor had assured her she was in fine physical condition and should breeze right through a perfectly normal pregnancy.

Still, it was a daunting prospect to raise a child on one's own. Yet other women did it. And actually her work wouldn't interfere. She could just as well read manuscripts at home as in the office. Sam would understand. Of course she could do it!

The telephone was ringing when she let herself in her house. Still stunned, she walked slowly over to answer it. As she'd expected, it was Laura.

'Well? What did he say?'

'It's true.'

There was a long silence. Rachel just stood there, holding the receiver in her hand, waiting for what she knew was coming. Might as well let Laura get it off her chest and be done with it.

'I suppose,' came her sister's voice at last, 'you haven't considered telling Stephen.'

Rachel sighed. 'No, Laura, I haven't. And I'm not going to.'

'I don't see why,' came the tart reply. 'After all, he's the father. He has to take some responsibility. In fact, knowing him, he'd insist on it, even if it was just financial help. He can well afford to.'

'Listen to me, Laura,' Rachel said when she finally could get a word in edgeways. 'I'm warning you right now that, sister or not, if you tell Stephen I'm pregnant I'll never speak to you again. I really mean it this time.'

'Yes,' Laura replied slowly. 'I can see that you do. Well, what are your plans?'

'Well, to tell you the truth I haven't really grasped the fact of the whole thing quite yet.' She laughed drily. 'I mean, it's one thing to think something dreadful might happen, but quite another to have one's worst fears confirmed officially. I don't know. I have to think about it.'

'Well, darling, I meant what I said. We'll do whatever we can to help you. Whatever you'll let us do, that is.'

'I know that. And thanks. Now, I think a long, relaxing soak in a hot bath is what I need more than anything. I'll talk to you later.'

After they hung up, Rachel walked slowly down the hall to the bedroom. As she ran the water in the tub and got undressed, she thought over her conversation with her sister. It had gone pretty much as she'd anticipated, but in the end Laura had seemed willing to take her at her word and not tell Stephen. Although Laura tended to interfere, she did always keep her promises.

As she stepped into the tub and lay back, closing her eyes, the fleeting thought crossed her mind that Laura could be right. Maybe she should tell Stephen. She was also right in thinking that he was the kind of man who would want to do his duty by her and the child. But even if he did decide he wanted to marry her again for the sake of being a real father to their child, that didn't mean he wanted *her*. And if she told him, wouldn't it amount to a form of blackmail?

She lay there thinking and getting nowhere until the water cooled, and ended up no closer to a solution than she'd been before.

In the morning, she still hadn't decided what to do about Stephen, but her mind was firmly made up about one thing. After an unappetising breakfast of dry crackers and a cup of lukewarm tea, which was all her churning stomach could manage, she called Sam at the office.

'Overton Publishing,' came Martha's cheerful voice.

'This is Rachel, Martha. Is Sam in yet?'

'He just walked in the door. Hang on a minute.'

In a few seconds Sam answered. 'Where are you, Rachel?' he said with no preamble. 'I need you here to help me decide on the artwork for the Helmerson book.'

'Sorry, Sam,' she said. 'I'm not feeling too hot this morning.'

'Oh,' he said, obviously taken aback. 'But you're never sick. What's wrong?'

'I think maybe I just have the blahs. You know, crashing down after all that intensive work I've had to put in with Lars over the past month. At any rate, I thought I'd take some time off.'

'But I *need* you!' he protested.

'No, you don't,' she replied firmly. 'I've done all I'm going to on that blasted book. I've worked every weekend, almost every evening on it, and I'm sick of it.'

'But it's a wonderful book!'

'I know,' she said with a sigh. 'But my job on it is over. I don't know anything about artwork, anyway. You and Lars will just have to figure out that aspect of it yourselves. I'm burned out, Sam. I need a rest.'

'How long?' he asked cautiously.

'I don't know. The rest of this week, anyway. Then next Monday I'll see how I feel. Right now, I just want to laze around for a few days, get my bearings again. I feel as though Lars and I have been off in never-never land for weeks, and I have a million things I need to catch up on.'

'Well, all right, then. I guess we can muddle along without you for a few days. And I can always call you if I get desperate.'

'No,' she said firmly. 'I'm going to unplug the telephone and just disappear for a while. I might even go out of town.'

There was a long silence. 'You really mean it, don't you?' he asked at last.

'I really do, Sam. You'll manage just fine without me.'

'Can I at least send you a few manuscripts to read? There were several new ones waiting on your desk this morning.' When she didn't reply, he went on hurriedly, 'But only if you feel like it, of course.'

'All right. You can send them to the house, but I'm not promising anything.'

'That's good enough for me. And Rachel?'

'Yes?'

'Take care of yourself. I don't want to lose you permanently.'

'No danger of that, Sam,' she said cheerfully.

No, she thought, as they said goodbye and hung up. She'd need that job more than ever now, with a child to raise on her own.

For the rest of that week, Rachel did exactly as she pleased for the first time in years, actually since she was a schoolgirl. She stayed up late and watched whatever idiotic programmes came on the television, then slept until mid-morning. She started reading through a stack of light paperback novels she'd accumulated and hadn't had the time to look at. She took naps in the afternoon, went for walks, pottered in the garden, and, although she did call Laura a few times, just so she wouldn't worry about her, she did unplug the telephone.

By the weekend, she was feeling more like herself again. Food tasted better, the mindless activities and adequate rest lulled her mind and improved her spirits, and she began to believe she actually could manage with a baby on her own. In fact, for the first time, the fact that at the end of it she would produce a child, a new human being in the world— Stephen's child—really sank in, and she found the prospect rather thrilling.

On Sunday night she decided to make a start on the package of manuscripts Sam had sent her. After dinner, she had a leisurely bath, put on nightgown, robe and slippers, settled herself at the kitchen table with a fresh pot of coffee and started to unwrap the parcel with something like her old sense of excited anticipation.

She had just opened the cover of the first manuscript when the front doorbell rang. Frowning, she perked up her ears, listening, hoping whoever it was would just go away. It had been so pleasant not to have to talk to anyone these past several days. Besides, there was no law that she had to answer her own doorbell. It was probably only Sam anyway, and she'd already warned him she didn't want to be disturbed.

It kept on ringing, and she kept on ignoring it, until finally there came a loud banging on the door. For a moment she was tempted to call the police. It would serve Sam right. But she knew she couldn't do that. She would, however, get rid of him right away and certainly wouldn't let him in.

With a sigh, she got to her feet and went to answer the door, a scathing comment already formed in her mind to deliver to Sam. When she opened it, however, and saw Stephen standing there, the words died on her lips, and all she could do was stare.

CHAPTER NINE

His face was livid, his eyes wild as he stood there for a second glaring at her. Then, abruptly, he pushed past her and kicked the door shut behind him. Rachel clutched the openings of her robe tighter, still too stunned to utter a word. He whirled around, still glaring, then came up to her and stood there looming over her.

'Why didn't you tell me you were going to have a baby?' he bit out at last.

By now she was over the shock of his unexpected appearance and had recovered her composure enough to speak. 'How did you find out?'

He waved a hand dismissively in the air. 'What difference does that make?'

She tied her robe more securely, then turned away from him. '*Damn* Laura, anyway,' she muttered. 'She *promised* me.'

'It wasn't Laura.'

She turned around, bewildered. 'But no one else knew.'

He gave her a thin, humourless smile. 'She didn't promise not to tell John.'

'Well,' she said with a toss of her head, 'it doesn't matter. You were bound to find out sooner or later. Now, just tell me why you're here, and then you can leave.'

'I came to ask you one question.'

'What is it?'

In spite of herself, once Rachel had taken in the fact that he was actually here, that he knew about the baby, was concerned, a little spark of hope had flickered into life inside her. And hadn't she known, deep down, that Laura would quite naturally tell John, would probably even put him up to informing Stephen that Rachel was going to have his child?

'There's only one reason I can figure out that you didn't tell me about it yourself,' he was saying now.

'That's not a question.'

'No. But this is.' His flinty grey eyes held her, as though they could see into the secret recesses of her very soul. 'I just need to know one thing. Is it my child?'

She reared her head back as though he had actually struck her. That he could even imagine it was another man's child simply took her breath away, and for a moment she couldn't utter a word, could only stand there, wide-eyed, staring up at him.

Then a slow flush of anger rose up in her, almost choking her. Her hand itched to slap the superior, accusing look off his face, to let him know how it felt to be suddenly brutally punished like that. Instead, she fought down the hot anger and deliberately calmed her mind and body into an icy cold.

Then she raised herself up to her full height and gave him a withering look that would have cowed a lesser man. 'That's the most insulting thing anyone has ever said to me, Stephen. I never would have thought it of you.'

For a moment he seemed quite startled, even a little abashed. Then, frowning, he lowered his head and stared down at the floor for several long moments. When he looked up at her again, his face was still stony, but there was a softer light in his eyes.

'I think it was a reasonable enough question,' he said quietly.

She raised questioning eyebrows. 'Do you?' she enquired sarcastically. 'Well, I have to wonder why you're even interested. It's been weeks since I've heard a word from you.'

'Well, if it is my child I feel responsible. I mean, I want to help you any way I can.'

'You mean financially,' she said.

'Well, yes, and, well . . .' He broke off and ran a hand over his dark hair. 'Listen, Rachel,' he said. 'John told me about it today at lunch. It's all new to me—a shock, actually—and I haven't really had time to digest it. I tried to call you, but when you didn't answer I decided to come over and discuss it with you, hopefully on a reasonable basis.'

She glared at him. 'And this is what you call reasonable?' she demanded. 'Barging in here and asking me a question like that?'

'A question I think I have every right to ask,' he replied loftily.

She could feel her frozen calm slipping away, but couldn't help herself. 'No!' she cried. 'You don't! You have no rights at all as far as I'm concerned.'

She narrowed her eyes at him. 'Remember, Stephen, you were the one who stormed out of here two weeks ago without giving me a chance to explain about Lars, and now you have the unmitigated gall to come here and accuse me of—of—having cheap affairs with other men.' Beside herself with fury by now, she was almost shouting, didn't care what she said. 'If I wouldn't sleep with you without being married, what makes you think I would with anyone else?'

'All right,' he said, raising a hand in the air to stem the tide. 'Calm down.'

'I will *not* calm down,' she stated, stamping her foot in sheer frustration. 'This is really the last straw, Stephen. As far as I'm concerned we have nothing to discuss.'

'Then it isn't mine.'

This only escalated her anger. 'I want you to leave now,' she said, and with a shaking finger pointed dramatically at the door.

'You don't mean that.'

'Oh, but I do.'

Their eyes locked together again, and this time she met his steely gaze unflinchingly. Watching the way his mouth was working, the little pulse along his jaw throbbing, she knew he was as angry as she was, but she would not back down. Not this time. She'd done all the retreating she was going to do.

'Come on, Rachel,' he said at last. 'Can't we just talk it over like sensible human beings?'

'No!' she shot out. 'Obviously we can't, not if you're going to start out by insulting me. I want you to go. Just get out. Now. Get out of my house and out of my life.'

'All right,' he said at last in a defeated tone. 'I'll go.'

He turned from her and walked slowly towards the door, as though waiting for her to call him back. She had to bite her lip until she could taste blood on it to keep from doing just that. Already regretting her harsh words, she still couldn't quite bring herself to take them back.

Ever since he'd come back into her life, he'd been calling all the shots, like a cat playing with a mouse, and she'd done all the backing down, all the apologising. In typical male fashion, he seemed to be convinced that ultimately, if he played his cards cleverly enough, he'd be able to have her and his freedom too. And she'd been willing to go along with him! Ready to take him on any terms she could get him.

Now, all that was changed. She had another person to consider—her child. And he had the gall to come barging over here with his suspicions that another man was its father.

When he was gone, she slid slowly down to the floor, resting her head back against the wall. She shut her eyes tight and held her breath, still resisting the temptation to call him back. She didn't move, didn't even breathe until she heard him drive away.

Then, at last, it was safe to let go. Cradling her head in her arms, she allowed the tears to flow unchecked.

*   *   *

The next morning, first thing, she called Laura. Although she was still furious at Stephen, a lot of her anger was aimed at her sister, and she intended to let her know just how she felt.

'Thanks a lot,' she said when Laura answered the telephone.

'What?' Laura mumbled sleepily. 'Is that you, Rachel? I just got up.'

'I just want to thank you for spilling the beans to Stephen, the way you promised you wouldn't.'

'But I didn't!' Laura protested.

'You told John. Knowing, I might add, he'd tell Stephen. Probably even prompting him to.'

'Oh, Rachel, come on, be reasonable. I promised you I wouldn't tell Stephen you were pregnant, and I didn't. And yes, I did tell John. But can't you get it through your head, you ninny, that we only want to help you? You act as though I did it to punish you or give myself a treat or something.'

'Well, you helped me, all right,' Rachel retorted. 'He came storming over here last night, just as you figured he would. But what you didn't count on was that his only motive was to find out if it was his child!'

There was a long silence. 'Oh, no,' Laura breathed at last. 'How stupid can such a smart man be? Please don't be mad at me, Rachel. It never entered my head he'd even question that.'

'Oh, I know that,' Rachel said wearily. 'I could hardly believe it myself. And no, I'm not really mad at you, not any more. I'm probably just taking it out on you for what he did.'

'What did you tell him?' Laura asked cautiously.

'I ordered him out of the house.'

'I see. Er—couldn't you just have told him the truth?'

'No! I couldn't! If he could even think such a thing, it's hopeless. Let him wonder. It won't hurt him.'

'But it might hurt you,' Laura said quietly.

Rachel gave a harsh laugh. 'I don't see what more can happen than already has. I'm in such a mess now that there's no way it could get any worse.'

'You haven't tried to raise a child on your own yet, my dear,' Laura replied tartly. 'And, as far as his wanting to know whether it's his child goes, that proves he still cares, doesn't it?'

'How do you figure that?'

'Well, he's obviously jealous. Listen, Rachel, I still think you and Stephen could make a go of it if you'd both bend just a little, think of the child's welfare instead of your own precious wounded egos. You're going to need all the help you can get.'

'Well, let me tell you the help he offered. If he can be assured it *is* his child, he wants to help me financially.'

'And that's it?'

'That's it.'

'Well, give him a little time to get used to the idea. After all, he only learned about it yesterday. He always wanted children, didn't he?'

Rachel heaved a deep sigh. 'To tell you the truth, Laura, I have no idea what he wants any more. I don't even know him.'

'Well, you have to do what you think best. I'm just going to give you one last parting bit of advice, then I'll never say another word about it. All right?'

'Oh, go ahead. You will anyway.'

'I think when he's had a chance to think things over he'll want to do the right thing and will be back. When he does, you've got to bury your pride, consider the child's welfare first, and at least talk things over with him.'

'Point taken, dear,' Rachel replied. 'You're probably right. Except for one thing.'

'What's that?'

'If I know Stephen, he won't be back.'

But as it turned out, she was quite wrong about that. It was the following Saturday morning, and she was out in front staking up the dahlias after a night of pouring rain that had beaten them down flat on the ground.

When his car pulled up out in front, she rose slowly to her feet, the stakes and twine still in her hands, watching as he got out of the car and came walking slowly up the path towards her. As he came closer she was struck by how tired he looked.

'Hello, Stephen,' she said when he reached her.

'Hello, Rachel,' he said. He hesitated for a moment, then asked, 'Do you suppose we could go inside and talk?'

She was about to refuse, to tell him that they'd said everything they needed to a week ago, but then she recalled the conversation she'd had with Laura, and she stopped herself just in time. Maybe he did deserve a chance to do the right thing. As the child's father, he also probably should shoulder some of the responsibility for it.

Besides all that, he looked so dear to her that she couldn't find it in her heart to resist him. He stood there like a chastened schoolboy, his hands stuck in the back pockets of his dark trousers, looking as though he hadn't slept for a week. His face was troubled, the grey eyes clouded over, with dark shadows under them. He hadn't shaved that morning, and a light stubble darkened his chin and jaws.

'All right,' she said at last. 'I guess the dahlias can wait.' She set down the stakes and twine. 'How about a cup of coffee?'

The relief on his face was quite evident. 'Sounds good.'

In the kitchen she washed her grimy hands at the sink and started to make the coffee, all the while intensely aware of him prowling around the room behind her. He seemed nervous, restless—a far cry from the confident, self-assured man she was so used to.

'The garden looks nice,' he said at last, breaking the tense silence.

She turned around. He was gazing out of the window, his back towards her. Even his broad shoulders were slumped forward in an attitude of defeat. It occurred to her then that although he had hurt her in the past, she hadn't been exactly all sweetness and light to him at all times, and her heart went out to him.

She laughed nervously. 'Well, I try, but it does tend to get ahead of me, especially this time of year, when everything seems to be growing out of control.'

The coffee had dripped through by now. She poured out two mugs and carried them over to the table.

'Coffee's ready,' she said.

He turned around and came slowly over to the table, picked up one of the mugs. After a quick sip, he set it back down and stood there staring blankly down at it for several moments. Finally he raised his eyes to hers.

'How are you feeling?' he asked.

'Great,' she replied. 'Although I was a little rocky at first. I think I just needed a good rest. I've taken the past week or so off, and may take another.'

He nodded absently. 'That's good.' He ran a hand over the back of his neck and down along the line of his jaw, frowning. 'I've been doing a lot of thinking this past week,' he said at last. 'And the first thing I want to do is apologise to you for the things I said, for implying...' He broke off with a shrug. 'Well, that you'd been fooling around, that some other man might be the child's father.'

'Well, I did think you knew me better than that,' she said. 'And I probably owe you an apology too for some of the things I said. You just made me very angry.'

He nodded. 'I know. It was just that when John told me you were pregnant, all I could think of was that you hadn't told me yourself, that I had to hear it from him. I saw red, and my first stupid thought was that possibly the reason you hadn't told me was because it wasn't mine.' He gave her a pleading look. 'If I'd waited a while, simmered down, really thought the thing through, I wouldn't have come barging over here the way I did.' His jaw tightened. 'Actually, if you want the truth, all I could think of was that blasted writer, seeing you two wrapped around each other that day.'

'If you had only let me explain about it then——'

'I know, I know,' he broke in. 'I was just blind with jealousy. It's that simple.'

She laughed drily. 'Well, I know how *that* feels,' she said. 'After all, it was my own jealousy that wrecked our marriage in the first place.'

'Not entirely,' he said quietly.

She shrugged. 'Well, that's all ancient history. No use assigning blame any more. Maybe we've both learned something.'

'That's really what I wanted to talk to you about today.'

He raised his mug, took a long swallow, then set it down and came around the table to stand before her. As she looked up at him, waiting, her heart began to pound wildly. Did he still want her? Did she want him? If he touched her now, she knew she'd be lost, would agree to anything.

But he didn't touch her. Instead he began to speak, slowly and carefully. 'What I think is that we both have a responsibility to the child—to our

child—and that means putting our personal griev-
ances behind us.'

'Yes,' she said. 'I agree.'

'You know I've always wanted children,' he went
on. 'And to me that doesn't mean weekend visi-
tation privileges, hovering on the fringes of its life.
I want to be a real father, an integral part of raising
it. So, I have a suggestion.'

She waited, but he didn't go on. It was as though
he was being very cautious, testing the waters,
feeling his way along, trying to gauge her reaction
before continuing.

'All right,' she said at last. 'What is it?'

'I think we should get married.'

For a moment, her heart soared, but in the next
second it plunged down with a dull thud. No, 'I
love you, Rachel; I can't live without you.'
Apparently he was willing to give up his precious
freedom, stick his head in the marital noose he'd
vowed to avoid at all costs, but not for her. It was
so he could be a father.

She bit her lip and turned away from him. Would
that be enough for her? How much should one be
expected to sacrifice for the sake of a child? And
would a loveless marriage even be good for it?

'Rachel?' he called softly to her. 'What do you
think?'

She turned back to him. 'I don't know, Stephen,'
she said slowly. 'You've been so set against marriage that you even had me convinced it wouldn't
work. I mean, a second marriage is risky enough,

but without love it seems to me it could be a disaster.'

His eyes flew open. 'Without love?' he exclaimed in utter astonishment. Then he frowned. 'Are you trying to tell me you don't care for me? That it's too late?'

'No. Not exactly.'

He spread his hands wide. 'Well, then, what exactly is it?' he asked in an exasperated tone. Then a light seemed to dawn. 'You're not doubting that I love you, are you?'

She flushed deeply. 'Well, what do you expect, Stephen?' she demanded hotly. 'First you tell me you don't believe in second marriages, then, just because I'm going to have a baby, you come here wanting to do the honourable thing. What am I supposed to think?'

He shook his head slowly from side to side, a look of total disbelief on his face. 'I don't see how you can doubt that it's you I want, you I love. The child is only a bonus.'

'But you said——'

'Oh, damn what I said!' he barked. He put his hands in his pockets and began pacing around the room.

As she watched him, her heart soared again, this time with real hope. Her every instinct was to go to him, to tell him how much she loved him, that of course she'd marry him, wanted to spend the rest of her life with him more than anything else in the world. But she stopped herself. She had to be sure.

Finally he came back to her. 'I said a lot of things I guess I really didn't mean. Actually, although I honestly didn't realise it at the time, I think I came to Seattle in the first place to try to get you back. I was so angry at your pig-headed refusal to believe me about Margaret and the way you rushed into the divorce that I wanted to punish you in some way. I don't know. Then, when I saw you, all that changed.'

He reached out and put a hand on her cheek. 'That one weekend we had together was so perfect, better even than what we had before. I knew then I was hooked good and proper, but I was still afraid to make a commitment. My idea was to take it slow, see how things worked out between us.' His jaw tightened. 'Then you delivered your little shocker about just being friends.'

'But I couldn't help that!' she protested. 'I knew by then, after that weekend, that it had to be all or nothing between us. Can't you see? An affair would have killed me.'

'Yes. I do see that now. I think I must have realised it even then. It's why I asked you to go to London with me. I had it half planned in my mind to get married before we went.'

'Well, why didn't you say so?'

'Because you chose to stay here with that damned Viking instead of going with me, that's why!'

She gazed up at him helplessly. What was the point of going on, of rehashing all the misunderstandings, the mistakes they'd both made? What mattered now was the future. He really did love her! Really did want her! Nothing else mattered. It was time to stop this futile parrying.

She took a step towards him. Slowly she raised a hand and placed it on his cheek, the stubble prickling against her palm. He was gazing down at her, the silvery eyes alight.

'Rachel,' he said in a hoarse voice. 'I'm begging, if that's what you want. Marry me. I want you. I want the chance to take care of you, of you and our child. Say you will.'

'Oh, Stephen,' she breathed, and threw her arms around his neck. 'Of course I will.'

His arms came around her then, and he held her tightly to him, all along the length of his lean, hard body, as though afraid to let go of her for an instant. They stood that way for some moments, locked together. Gradually, Rachel could feel the heat generating between them, and the embrace took on a different character.

His hands were moving up and down her back, clutching at her hips, pulling her up even more closely against his lower body, and she could tell that what he was feeling now was far more desire than gratitude.

'God, how I want you, darling,' he breathed into her ear. 'I've never stopped wanting you.' He held her face in his hands and gazed down deeply into her eyes. 'I love you so much, more than my life.'

She pulled her head back to look up into the grey depths, which were glittering now with love, love for *her*. 'I know,' she breathed. 'And I love you, too.'

His mouth came down on hers hungrily, greedily, then in a demanding, open-mouthed kiss. Rachel responded ardently, clutching at him, sliding her hands up under the thin knit shirt to run them over the smooth skin of his back.

Finally he tore his mouth away and smiled down at her. 'Come on,' he said, taking her by the hand. 'Let's go and sit down. I want to make sure the air is cleared for good before...' He grinned. 'You know.'

She nodded happily, and they walked hand in hand into the living-room. He made straight for *his* chair, sat down, then pulled her down into his lap.

'Mmm,' he murmured, nuzzling her ear. 'You smell good.'

She laughed. 'I smell like a gardener!' she exclaimed. 'I've been digging in the dirt, remember?'

His arms were around her, holding her closely up against him, her head nestling on his broad shoulder. She laid her hand on his chest, just over his heart, which was pounding as rapidly as her own.

'Now,' he said huskily, 'we won't have any more misunderstandings, will we?'

'No,' she murmured with a shake of her head.

He was stroking her tawny hair, his lips on her forehead. 'And we've covered all the bases?'

She nodded wordlessly.

'We'll get married right away?' She nodded again. 'And be a real family?' Another nod. 'Ah,' he said with satisfaction. 'Then I think that takes care of everything.'

She raised her face to his and gave him a sly grin. 'Not quite everything,' she said.

He raised a questioning eyebrow. Their eyes met, and slowly the light dawned in the grey depths. 'Well,' he whispered, 'we can take care of that right now.'

He dipped his dark head towards her and their lips met in a long, lingering kiss of ineffable sweetness. She felt his hand slip under the loose hem of her blouse, then slide slowly up her bare back. As the kiss deepened and his tongue pushed into her eager mouth, the hand came around to brush against the sides of her breasts, then started fumbling with the buttons of her blouse.

When he was through, he pushed aside the openings and brushed his hand lightly, possessively across her breasts, so much fuller now since her pregnancy began, and she drew in a sharp breath at the touch. Slowly, he stroked one full mound, then the other, his fingers lingering over each taut peak, playing with them, teasing, until she could hardly bear the exquisite torment.

When he tore his mouth away from hers and bent his head lower, she threw her head back, giving herself up entirely to the thrill of his touch, his lips on her neck, then lower into the valley between her breasts, and then, at last, closing around first one thrusting nipple, then the other.

As his hot mouth did its work on her, his hands were undoing the fastening of her jeans, until he was able to slide one hand slowly, tantalisingly down over her stomach, then lower, over her thighs, barely touching her now, until she ached for more.

Finally she could bear no more. She sat up and raised her head, looking down deeply into his eyes. 'Let's go, darling,' she said. 'Let's go to bed.'

She got up off his lap and started towards the door, but before she'd gone a step he came up behind her, his hands tugging at her shirt, pulling it off over her shoulders. Then, he stooped down and pulled her jeans down over her legs until she stood naked before him. His hands came back to cover her breasts, kneading and stroking from one pulsating peak to the other. She leaned back against him, lost in desire.

He raised his hands and shrugged out of his shirt. Then, when he started to unbuckle his belt, she reached out a hand to stop him. 'No,' she breathed. 'Let me.'

He let his hands fall to his sides and stood there, grey eyes glittering, as she reached out to finish undoing the belt, then, raising her hands and placing them flat on his smooth chest, she slowly slid them down until they reached the low waistband of his dark trousers. As she slipped her hand inside, down over the matting of coarse hair, she heard him moan softly, deep in his throat.

Finally he groaned loudly, reached down, and drew her up to enfold her in his arms again. 'If you don't stop, my darling, it's going to be over before it starts.' He pulled down the trousers the rest of the way, stepped out of them, then reached down and swooped her up into his arms. 'Come on, we're going to bed.'

In the bedroom, he laid her down carefully on top of the bed, then stood by the side of it, gazing down at her for a long moment, while she stared up lovingly at his naked body, hard and strong, so different from her own.

She reached out her arms for him at last. 'Come to me, Stephen,' she breathed.

He settled himself on the bed, braced on his elbows, hovering over her, then slowly lowered himself on top of her. 'I'm not too heavy, am I, darling?' he asked.

'No. Don't move an inch away.'

She gazed up at him as his mouth opened wide, then came down hotly on hers, his body grinding into hers. He broke away and moved his hands and lips down the length of her body, lingering over each breast to torment it even more, then her abdomen, her thighs, her calves, then back up again.

Finally she could bear no more. Tugging at his shoulders, she pulled him up so that he loomed over her. 'Now, Stephen,' she said.

He kissed her then, his mouth hot on hers, his breath coming in short, laboured rasps, his hard need pressing into her. She shifted her body under his until they were joined together and reached the heights of love at last.

Some time later, Rachel awoke beside the man she'd never stopped thinking of as her husband. She opened her eyes and raised her head up a little off the pillow to see that the sun was still shining. It must still be morning.

Stephen stirred in his sleep, shifting his weight so that he was turned towards her now, his hand clasping her around the waist, then moving up to settle on her bare breast. She lay back down with a sigh of contentment, put her hand over his, pressing it closer over her heart, and smiled to herself.

Everything would be all right, she mused happily. Stephen had said they'd be a real family now, something he'd always wanted, what she realised now she'd always wanted, too. She could continue with her work, and in time perhaps they'd have another child.

She turned her head to look at him. His face was relaxed in sleep, the dark, thick eyelashes resting on his high cheeks, the fine mouth slightly open, the black hair tousled. She longed to reach over and smooth it back, but didn't want to disturb him.

Yes, she thought happily, gazing her fill at the sleeping man, it was just like old times. Only better, infinitely better. Through their pain, they'd both learned what was really important in life. It wasn't pride, it wasn't riches or success.

All it took was love.

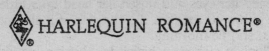

HARLEQUIN ROMANCE®

brings you

More Romances Celebrating Love, Families and Children!

Harlequin Romance #3362

THE BABY BUSINESS

by

Rebecca Winters

If you love babies—this book is for you!

When hotel nanny Rachel Ellis searches for her lost brother, she meets his boss—the dashing and gorgeous Vincente de Raino. She is unprepared for her strong attraction to him, but even more unprepared to be left holding the baby—his adorable baby niece, Luisa, who makes her long for a baby of her own!

Available in May wherever Harlequin Books are sold.

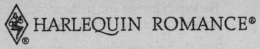

 HARLEQUIN ROMANCE®

celebrates

FAMILY TIES!

Join us in June for our brand-new miniseries—
Family Ties!

Family... What does it bring to mind? The trials and
pleasures of children and grandchildren, loving parents
and close bonds with brothers and sisters—that special
joy a close family can bring. Whatever meaning it has for
you, we know you'll enjoy these heartwarming love stories
in which we celebrate family—and in which you can
meet some fascinating members of our
heroes' and heroines' families.

The first title to look out for is...
Simply the Best
by Catherine Spencer

followed by...

Make Believe Marriage
by Renee Roszel in July

FT-G-R